Wyckford General Hospital

Small-town medics finding big love!

There must be something in the water in Wyckford, Massachusetts. The small and quirky town is brimming with dedicated medics and first responders who are at the top of their game.

The one thing they don't have is love. Some have had it and then lost it, some wanted to find themselves first and some have never felt they could have it—until now. They're all about to find themselves fighting to resist temptation—the temptation to have everything they've ever wanted!

Discover Brock and Cassie's story in

Single Dad's Unexpected Reunion

Available now!

And look out for the other
Wyckford General Hospital stories

Coming soon!

Dear Reader,

When imagining the setting for *Single Dad's Unexpected Reunion*, I wanted to place these characters somewhere in New England, near Boston. My family, generations ago, had owned land near Buzzards Bay. Not only is it a fun name to play with, but the connection was too much to resist. My fictional town of Wyckford, Massachusetts, is filled with lots of colorful characters I hope you'll enjoy reading about!

Cassie is a woman who chose to leave her hometown behind to get over her feelings for an unrequited crush and build a new life for herself in California. But when she returns to Wyckford after giving a presentation at a conference in Boston, one of the first people she sees is her old crush, Dr. Brock Turner. Our hero's been dealing with heartache himself the last five years after losing his wife and parents and raising his daughter, Adi, alone. Now that Cassie's back and working with him on a case, he's learning his connection with her is unexpected and unforgettable.

If you love second chances, opposite attraction, single dads, forced proximity and plenty of sizzling chemistry between your leads, *Single Dad's Unexpected Reunion* is for you!

Happy reading!

Traci <3

SINGLE DAD'S UNEXPECTED REUNION

TRACI DOUGLASS

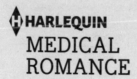

MEDICAL ROMANCE

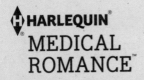

Recycling programs
for this product may
not exist in your area.

ISBN-13: 978-1-335-59489-1

Single Dad's Unexpected Reunion

Harlequin Enterprises ULC
22 Adelaide St. West, 41st Floor
Toronto, Ontario M5H 4E3, Canada
www.Harlequin.com

Printed in U.S.A.

Traci Douglass is a *USA TODAY* bestselling romance author with Harlequin, Entangled Publishing and Tule Publishing and has an MFA in Writing Popular Fiction from Seton Hill University. She writes sometimes funny, usually awkward, always emotional stories about strong, quirky, wounded characters overcoming past adversity to find their forever person and heartfelt, healing happily-ever-afters. Connect with her through her website: tracidouglassbooks.com.

Books by Traci Douglass

Harlequin Medical Romance

First Response in Florida
The Vet's Unexpected Hero
Her One-Night Secret

Their Hot Hawaiian Fling
Neurosurgeon's Christmas to Remember
Costa Rican Fling with the Doc
Island Reunion with the Single Dad
Their Barcelona Baby Bombshell
A Mistletoe Kiss in Manhattan
The GP's Royal Secret

Visit the Author Profile page at Harlequin.com.

To all my faithful readers,

Thank you for reading my stories and allowing me to continue doing what I love to do!

And to my amazing editor, Charlotte,

Thank you for always having my back and helping me make my books into something people want to read!

<3

Praise for
Traci Douglass

"*Their Hot Hawaiian Fling* by Traci Douglass is a fantastic romance…. I love this author's medical romance books and this is no exception. Both characters are well written, complex, flawed and well fleshed out. The story was perfectly paced. A great romance I highly recommend."

—*Goodreads*

CHAPTER ONE

"AND IN CONCLUSION, I believe the expedited use of our innovative virtual planning and three-dimensional printing METAMORPHOSIS technology will allow this process to improve treatment outcomes in acute facial trauma cases by bringing the entire team—surgeons, radiologists, biomedical engineers and designers—in at the initial point of care to revolutionize the field of craniomaxillofacial surgery. Thank you."

Dr. Cassandra Murphy smiled politely at the room full of the country's top plastic surgeons to whom she'd given her presentation at the Westin Copley Square Hotel in Boston. It was the first time she'd been back in her home state since leaving Massachusetts for her new job in California more than five years prior, and she was still sorting through her feelings on that matter. She gathered her notes and headed down the stairs amidst a flurry of handshakes and well-wishes from her esteemed colleagues.

She'd gone to San Diego to change her life all those years ago, and she'd done it. As the youngest partner in her practice, Cassie had the opportunity to stay on the cutting edge of her profession, which was what had brought her back here today to speak at the national annual conference on plastic and reconstructive surgery. This was the last day of the four-day event, and she'd planned to spend a little extra time in the area to see her father, an ex-commercial fisherman who'd recently moved into a retirement home. Also, the new administrator at the local hospital in her hometown, Wyckford General, had asked Cassie to consult on a patient there. A young woman who'd been in a car accident six months prior who might be a good candidate for the new technology Cassie had just given her presentation on.

As the MC announced the second speaker on the day's roster, Cassie exited the ballroom and headed for the lobby to check out. An hour and a half later, exhausted, edgy and reconsidering the wisdom of her choice to drive home to Wyckford, Massachusetts after a long, hectic couple of days—Cassie slid into a back booth at the tiny Buzzy Bird diner and sagged against the red vinyl seat. It had been years since she'd been back, and yet it felt like yesterday.

"Cassie!" a female voice called. She turned to

see her good friend Madison Scott. She'd kept in contact with several of her besties when she'd moved west, and they kept her up to date on all things Wyckford gossip and on her father, who tended to just tell Cassie everything was "fine."

Madi was an ER nurse at Wyckford General Hospital and based on her wrinkled scrubs and the shadows under her eyes, she'd just pulled another all-night shift. She walked over and gave Cassie a big hug before scooting into the other side of the booth. "Wow. You look amazing, Cass. Life in California must agree with you."

"Hey, stranger. Long time no see." This came from the third member of their group, Luna Norton. She wore a black T-shirt, black pants and pink Chuck Taylors. A white apron emblazoned with a cartoon buzzard completed her look. In addition to working as a physical therapist, Luna also helped part-time at the diner her family owned. It was just like old times and reminded Cassie of how little things had changed in Wyckford. Well, most things, anyway. Luna also gave Cassie a hug then asked, "What do you guys want to drink before we catch up?"

"Hot tea, please. Green, if you have it," Cassie said, fighting a yawn. With all the prep she'd done last night for her presentation this morning, plus teleconferencing with the other physicians in her practice about her patients back in

San Diego, Cassie hadn't gotten much sleep the night before. "And a scone, please."

"Coffee for me," Madi said. "The stronger, the better. And bring a whole plate of scones."

Luna smiled. "Be right back."

Minutes later, Luna reappeared with their order and set it all on the table before taking a seat in the booth beside Madi, across from Cassie. "Feels good to sit down. I've been on my feet since eight this morning."

"Join the club," Madi said. "Except add twelve hours onto that for me."

"Seems like we've all had a busy day." Cassie smiled, not missing the long hours and nonstop adrenaline rush of her resident days in Boston. She'd put her time and energy into graduating at the top of her class in medical school, then taken an opportunity on the West Coast to make a fresh start. A new beginning away from Wyckford and away from the man she'd had an impossible crush on who'd never even known she'd existed. Not romantically, anyway.

Dr. Brock Turner.

He'd been a fellow resident and all-around golden boy. His father had a successful GP practice in Wyckford. Brock had done a double specialty in medical school—GP and Trauma Surgery—and from what Madi and Luna had told her over the years, Brock had eventually taken over his father's practice after his parents had been killed in a car accident a few years ago. Unfortunately, that hadn't been the only loss that poor Brock had suffered. He'd also lost his beloved wife prior to his parents' passing, also in a car accident, during a bad ice storm. She wondered how much grief had affected the man she'd once admired from afar. Back when she'd known him, Brock Turner was funny and smart and charming, winning friends and admirers with his movie-star looks and easy smile.

Cassie had been the opposite in medical school—shy and nerdy, doing her best to learn everything she could to make something of herself. Her mom had died of cancer when Cassie was only five, and her father, Ben Murphy, had worked hard to raise his daughter alone and saved all the money he made as a commercial fisherman to pay for Cassie's college. She hadn't wanted to let him down. Not after he'd devoted so much to her.

So she'd studied and worked and basically kept her head down and her eyes on the prize of graduation and being a doctor. And if she sometimes fantasized that Brock Turner would suddenly fall for her and profess his undying love, well, no harm done. Cassie hadn't been silly enough to think he'd look twice her way back then. Not with his gorgeous, and equally sweet, girlfriend Kylie by his side. Talk about a blessed couple. Right before Cassie had decided to leave for California after medical school, Brock and Kylie had announced their engagement.

Cassie sipped her tea and glanced out the window at Buzzards Bay across the street from the diner. Her heart ached for Kylie, who'd drowned in the very same bay Cassie was looking at now. She still remembered hearing about it from Madi and Luna. There'd been wicked slick weather that night, and Kylie's car had slid on the ice and crashed into the water. By the time rescuers had reached her, it'd been too late. Cassie still shuddered thinking about how awful that must've been for Brock. Losing his wife and having a newborn baby to take care of on his own.

Setting her tea down to grab a scone, Cassie took a bite of the still-warm-from-the-oven cinnamon chip goodness and couldn't resist a groan of pleasure. "These are so amazing, Luna."

"Thanks." Luna took one herself from the plate and bit into it, never one to waste her break.

Madi, who carefully sliced her scone in half with her knife instead of using her hands like her heathen friends, looked over at Cassie. "So how long are you in town?"

Cassie stilled for a beat. "Not sure. Depends on the case I'm consulting on. Could be a couple of weeks, could be more. I'll certainly be here long enough to see my dad and catch up with you guys though, then back to California."

For the past five years, she'd worked her ass off, running on the hamster wheel of their busy practice, heading toward the future she'd planned for herself as a successful plastic surgeon. She wanted to make her dad proud, wanted to make a name for herself. Wanted to live up to her own high ideals of achievement, then achieve higher. Perhaps then she could get rid of that knot of emptiness inside her. The one that had existed since the day her mother died.

"How'd your presentation go?" Madi asked.

"Good, thanks." She'd given her two-hour-long talk and had been honored to be part of something that would change patients' lives and revolutionize her field. Now, if she could get her personal life in the same stellar shape as her professional one, she'd be all set. Not that she had much time to devote to relationships, but maybe this trip could change that. Teach her how to slow down a bit…

She glanced out the window at the trees, their leaves bright green in the late morning rays of June sunshine, and thought maybe it was time to find something more when it came to love, scary as that sounded. Until now, she'd been too busy with work to have more than fleeting romances. It wasn't that she didn't want kids…*someday*.

But now it felt like someday was creeping closer than ever with each passing birthday. Or maybe that was just everyone around her settling down, and she didn't want to get left behind. Not to mention her dad kept bugging her about when she'd give him grandkids.

She'd rented a small vacation home online, hoping to enjoy some quiet time while she was here and fly under the local gossip radar, since the town of Wyckford and secrets went together like toothpaste and peanut butter. Gossip was their number two industry, after tourism.

"Well, we'll have to make the most of your visit then," Madi said.

Cassie smiled and took another bite of scone. From what she'd seen on her drive in, Wyckford was still small and quirky, with a population of just around twenty-four thousand. The kind of place where everyone knew everyone else's business. Another reason Cassie had been glad to leave after medical school. Hard to make a fresh start when the past haunted around every corner.

And make a fresh start, she had. Not just professionally, but physically. She'd always been slim and petite, but when she'd left her hometown, her hair had been mousy brown, and she'd worn thick glasses. Now, thanks to LASIK, she was glasses-free and, thanks to her fantastic stylist, her long hair rippled over her shoulders in shiny chestnut waves, highlighted with copper and gold. Her clothes were comfortable but expensive, tailored by the finest designer boutiques. And while she didn't flaunt her wealth, Cassie did more than all right for herself financially. She didn't need anyone to support her.

Not money-wise, anyway.

She finished her scone, then took another from the plate and bit into it. "Can't wait to see all my old favorite things in town."

Luna snorted. "Favorite things, huh? What about Brock Turner?"

Cassie frowned. "What about him?"

"Stop it." Madi gave Luna a scowling side glance. "I'm sure Cassie's forgotten all about him. Besides, he's so busy these days. He's got no time for anyone except himself and Adi and Riley. And she's here to have fun, not dredge up the past."

Cassie knew Riley was Brock's younger sister, who'd also been involved in the accident that had killed Brock's parents. Riley had survived, Cassie had heard, but with life-altering injuries. Adi must be Brock's daughter then. Her heart squeezed once more for what poor Brock and his family had been through. "How's he doing?"

Two hours later, they'd left the diner and Cassie was on her way to check in at her online rental when her phone buzzed. Her private cell number was the only thing that hadn't changed from her old Wyckford life. Easier to keep it, because of her dad, than to get a new one when she'd moved to California. She hit a button on the dash to connect the call through her rental SUV's Bluetooth and answered, not bothering to check the number, since the only people who ever called her on this phone were Madi and Luna or her father. Her colleagues from the practice used the phone the office gave her. But she wasn't on call during her trip, so that phone was tucked safely away in her luggage for now. "Hello?"

"I'm calling about your flyer," a man said. "I need a dog walker. Someone who's on time, responsible and not a flake."

Flyer? Cassie stopped for a red light, scowling at her dashboard display. "A dog walker?"

"Yes, and I need you to start immediately, if possible."

Wrong number. Cassie was about to tell the man so when something about his voice struck her as familiar. Low and a little raspy, with a hint of impatience…

No. It couldn't be.

She squinted at the number on the display but didn't recognize it, yet from the chord vibrating deep inside her, it had to be him. Dr. Brock

Turner. Her fantasy man from all those years ago. She'd never expected to see him during her time here—in fact, she'd actively planned to avoid it, if possible—but it seemed fate had intervened. Again. She needed to hang up, needed to get on with her visit and forget all about this man. She'd spent the last five years getting over her impossible crush on him and having anything to do with him now might undo all that hard work. No. Continuing with this call was a very bad idea.

Cassie was about to hang up when he continued, stopping her.

"Look, I had an early shift at the hospital this morning and won't be home until late tonight. I have a puppy at home who probably needs to potty bad. I just need someone to take her for a short walk to do her business. I'll pay twice the rate listed on your flyer for the last-minute inconvenience. Fifty dollars."

Oh, boy.

Low and authoritative, that voice of his had always made Cassie want to snap to attention and salute him, in a sexy way. The fact the rest of him was gorgeous too—tall, dark and delicious, with bright blue eyes to boot—well, it was a combination she couldn't resist.

Don't do it. Don't do it. Don't do it.

The logical part of her brain screamed that she

should stick to her plan. Avoid Brock Turner at all costs and get on with her life. But the emotional part of Cassie, her neglected heart that she'd come back to Wyckford to nurture and rediscover, said why not help the guy out? Besides, she was over him. That's what the past five years had been about. She was a different person now. Lord knew he was too, after all he'd been through. It was silly to avoid someone over something that had happened a long time ago. And Brock probably didn't even remember her, let alone know she'd had a crush on him. Wyckford wasn't that big anyway and walking his puppy wouldn't take more than a few minutes at best. He wouldn't even be there, since he'd said he was working late. She could confirm for herself how he was doing and then walk away clean.

Before she knew what had happened, Cassie had rationalized herself right into it.

"Fine. Where and when."

At the appropriate time, she pulled up to the address Brock had given her and took a deep breath, still slightly amazed at herself for choosing to do this. It was a bit crazy, agreeing to walk Brock's dog for him when he had no idea who was really on the other end of the line, but he needed help, and she needed the closure of knowing she was well and truly over the man.

Hopefully, this would take care of both problems in one fell swoop.

His house was stunning. Two-story, with an exterior that reminded Cassie of old-world European architecture, on a wooded lot right on the bay. The houses were spread out in this expensive area of town, with rocky beaches that stretched for endless miles and dark green bluffs and rock formations for as far as the eye could see.

She parked her SUV under the front portico and walked up to the door. A handwritten note was stuck to the glass.

Door's unlocked. Let yourself in then destroy this note. And don't tell Brock. He'll kill me if he knows I left his house open without the alarm set.

Riley

Cassie stared at the scrawled message from Brock's younger sister, trying to decide if she should actually go through with this or leave. Because now that she was here, on the threshold, all her earlier rationalizations fled, and this seemed like a bad idea. Especially since walking into his house without a key was problematic, at best. If not illegal, at worst.

She glanced around again to see if any nosy neighbors were watching. Getting arrested tonight was not on her career achievement plan. Then she looked down at her outfit—not exactly dog-walking attire. She'd not changed after her presentation earlier, so she was still wearing her crisp black business suit—a blazer and knee-length skirt—and black pumps. Not great for prowling or pounding the pavement.

From inside the house came a happy, high-pitched bark. Then another.

Okay. Fine. She was probably blowing this out of proportion. It was a quick dog walk. Nothing more. And Brock had asked her to come here and do it. If the cops showed up, she had that to fall back on. Plus, from the sounds of those barks and whines, his puppy had to go quite badly.

Cassie opened the front door and peered inside.

The interior of the home was as stunning as the outside. Wide open spaces, done in dark tones and neutral colors. The furniture was over-sized and sparse, and the floors were beautiful hardwood. An entire wall of windows faced the setting sun and Buzzards Bay.

As she stepped inside, the barking increased in volume. Cassie followed the sounds through a huge, state-of-the-art, open-style kitchen that made her wish she knew how to cook beyond the basics of soup and grilled cheese sandwiches.

Then to a laundry room, where the doorway was blocked by a toddler gate.

On the other side of it sat a tiny, adorable French bulldog.

Tan, with bat ears, large dark eyes and a tongue lolling out of the side of its mouth, the puppy looked like an animated cartoon as it twirled in excited circles, dancing for her, trying to impress and charm its way out of lockup.

"Hi there." Cassie crouched in front of the gate. The little dog—she hadn't gotten its name—snuffled against her hand, snorting in joyous delirium, rolling over so Cassie could scratch its belly, then jumping to its feet and hopping around again. Too cute.

"Let's get you out here so we can take a walk, huh?" Cassie grinned as she opened the gate, then fell back on her butt as the dog streaked past her like a bolt of lightning, racing through the kitchen and out of sight.

"Hey," she called, clambering back to her feet. "Come back. Let's go for a walk!"

But the puppy didn't, and wow, for something so tiny, it moved fast. The bulldog snorted with sheer delight as it ran circles around the couch, barking with merry enthusiasm. Cassie gave chase, but then the dog changed direction, heading back into the kitchen.

Giving up, she returned to the laundry room

and found a pink collar and leash hanging on a hook by the door. Embroidered on the collar was a name: Winnie.

Cassie laughed. Well, the dog certainly had the roly-poly, cuddly part down, that was for sure. She found Winnie sitting by the front door, panting, apparently having worn off all her excess energy.

"Good girl," Cassie cooed as she moved closer with the collar. "Want to go for a walk?"

Winnie gave her a goofy puppy grin.

Aw. See? She had made the right choice here. Cassie understood how exhausting being a busy physician was, having pulled many long shifts herself. Brock needed help, and she was glad to provide it. But before she could get the collar secured around Winnie's neck, the dog escaped through the still-open front door, tearing toward Buzzards Bay at breakneck speed.

Blood pounding in her ears, Cassie straightened and shouted, "Wait, Winnie. Stop!"

But Winnie didn't stop. The puppy hit the rocky beach and headed straight for the water.

"No!" Cassie yelled, in full panic mode now. "Stop!"

Tiny Winnie dived into the bay.

Cursing, Cassie ran after her, kicking off her fancy pumps along the way for better traction. She stopped at the water's edge, cold water nipping at her bare toes as she frantically searched for a bobbing head. Nothing. It seemed that Brock's puppy had vanished.

With the water inching closer to her ankles, Cassie staggered back, still searching.

Still nothing.

Her heart sank as she pulled her phone from her blazer pocket and hit redial for the number Brock had called from earlier. Pulse slamming against her temples and throat tight, she waited until he picked up.

"Dr. Turner," came his low, deep voice.

And just like that, Cassie was back in residency and hopelessly, horribly, head over heels for the man, even though she knew how completely ridiculous it was.

She could still picture him after a long shift in his wrinkled scrubs, his dark hair tousled, and his blue eyes lined with exhaustion. A movie-star build and a mind for science. Their gazes had locked a few times as they'd worked on patients together during rotations and, for Cassie at least, the air had fizzed with chemistry.

And now she'd lost the guy's puppy. The man who'd lost so much already.

"Um…hello," she said, her explanation tumbling out on a river of nerves and regret. "This is Dr. Cassandra Murphy. We were in residency together. I was the one you called earlier about walking your dog tonight, and I know it was a mistake, and I should have told you then that you had the wrong number, but…" She swallowed hard as she scanned the still empty horizon. "I wanted to help. And now it seems I've lost Winnie. Your puppy's gone."

Silence followed from the other end of the line.

"And I'm so sorry," Cassie added.

More silence.

Cassie huffed out a breath, leaned against a nearby boulder before her wobbly knees gave out, and ran a shaky hand through her hair. "Brock? Did you hear me?"

"Cassie Murphy?" he said quietly, as if still taking it in. "What the hell are you doing in Wyckford?"

She swallowed and gripped the phone tighter, still scanning the area for any sign of the dog. "I was in Boston for a medical conference and afterward I drove here to consult on a patient and spend some time relaxing and seeing family and friends."

"And lose my puppy," he added.

Cassie squeezed her eyes shut, shaking her head. "I'm so sorry. I thought I was helping—"

"And you're sure Winnie's gone?"

Cassie looked up and down the beach. The empty beach. "Yes."

"Then I should thank you."

Stunned at his heartless words, Cassie stared at her phone before putting it back to her ear, straightening once more as she scowled. "No. I don't think you understand. I *lost* your puppy. In the bay."

Brock muttered something Cassie didn't catch.

"Sorry?" She wasn't sure how long a dog could survive underwater, but chances were good that Winnie was in serious trouble. If she could just spot the puppy, she could pull it to shore. Cassie had never performed canine CPR, but it couldn't be that different. Cover the muzzle and breathe, chest compressions until help arrived.

"Stay there. I'm two minutes away," Brock said. "I had a break in the ER and decided to run home to make sure you showed up."

"Well, of course I showed—" she said, but he'd already ended the call.

Uncharacteristically flustered, Cassie slid her phone back into her pocket and searched again. According to Brock, she had two minutes to find Winnie, and she wasn't about to waste a second of it.

CHAPTER TWO

BROCK'S DAY HAD started at five that morning, working out at the gym with his closest friends—Mark Bates, a firefighter, and Tate Griffin, a local paramedic on the flight team for Wyckford General.

By six-thirty he was in his office at the GP his father had started, and which Brock was doing his best to keep afloat, going through patient files and gearing up for his day. Then he'd been called to the ER to consult on a guy who'd gotten in a drunken fight in Boston hours before and had a nasty cut on his face. Normally, the guy could've gone to an ER right in Beantown, but apparently the man had been so , he'd driven all the way back to Wyckford without even noticing he'd been covered in his own blood. The cops had waited at the man's bedside to arrest him and take him to jail as soon as Brock had finished. Sitting in a cell would give him plenty of recovery time. From there, Brock had moved on to a cardiac arrest victim and then to a three-year-old who'd swallowed a Lego and was having understandable trouble passing it.

By noon, Brock wasn't even halfway through his day, and he'd already been overloaded and overworked and was quite possibly teetering on the edge of burnout. He felt it creeping in on him in unguarded moments—like now, as he parked his car in his driveway to deal with the last person on earth he ever thought he'd see again.

Dr. Cassandra Murphy.

He still couldn't quite believe she was here in Wyckford. The last time he'd seen Cassie had been at the big Fourth of July fireworks show up in Boston when they'd still been residents. A bunch of them had gone as a last celebration before graduation. An image of Cassie from back then popped into his mind, her brown hair always pulled back in a ponytail, her eyes hidden behind the owlish glasses she always wore. Skinny and serious, she'd seemed to fade into the background. Of course, Brock had been so focused on his beautiful fiancée, Kylie, that he hadn't seen much else happening around him. He'd been totally in love and totally devoted. In fact, he and Kylie had announced their engagement at that same picnic. Six months later, they'd been married and celebrating the birth of their first kid.

Then tragedy had changed Brock's life forever.

Now, as he walked across the rocky shoreline toward the bay, he did his best to ignore the dull grief knotting his chest and instead concentrated on the woman standing near the water. Cassie faced the bay with her hands on her head, looking distraught.

As Brock picked up the pace, something dashed toward him in his peripheral vision. Something small and evil.

Winnie.

Brock scooped up the sand-covered puppy with one hand and held her away from him. The French bulldog wriggled with joy, still running in the air as she tried to get closer to him. Finally giving up, Winnie refocused her attention on the woman near the shore.

"Oh, I see her," Brock whispered to the dog. "And what the hell have you done now?"

Panic constricted Cassie's throat as she yelled once more. "Winnie!"

A yip sounded behind her, and she turned and froze.

Because there was Brock Turner. In a pair of blue scrubs and looking just as gorgeous as she remembered. In his arms was the puppy, who panted happily, as if she hadn't just given Cassie the fright of her life. In fact, if she didn't know better, she'd swear that dog was grinning.

Relieved, Cassie started toward them, only to trip over a small rock jutting out of the sand. So much for a dignified reunion. Before her knees hit the sand though, two big hands gripped her arms and kept her upright.

It took her a second to recover from the thrilling shock of Brock's touch before she pulled away from him. "I'm okay, thanks."

"Sure?"

"Yes. I'm good."

He nodded but didn't let her go.

Except…no. That wasn't right. Because it was *her* keeping hold of *him*, she realized. Her fingers gripping those solid biceps, soaking up his warmth and strength and—

Oops.

Forcing herself to let him go, Cassie stepped back and smoothed a hand down the front of her suit, searching for the long lost shreds of her dignity. Then she glanced up at Brock, tilting her head to see his face. She'd forgotten how tall he was. And based on their proximity, she could also see he hadn't shaved that morning. The dark stubble on his jaw made him somehow even sexier.

Winnie barked from the beach beside them where Brock had set her down, as if in agreement, before grabbing one of Cassie's expensive pumps that she'd discarded on the beach. The little dog growled, then began to gnaw on the heel.

Brock pulled the shoe away from Winnie, attempting to smooth out the dog's teeth marks with his thumb as Winnie moved on to the second pump.

Demon.

He nudged the puppy away and rescued the second shoe, doing his best to concentrate on the situation at hand and not the woman standing across from him. Cassie looked so different that it was stunning. In a good way. Gone was the mousy brown hair, replaced by shiny red and gold and dark chocolate tresses that made his hands itch to bury themselves in it. She'd filled out too, in all the right places. Those glasses had disappeared, revealing lovely hazel eyes. The overall effect was attractive. Very attractive.

Then there was her mouth. For some reason, he'd never noticed her mouth before today.

She had a full lower lip, one that raised his temperature and made him think about sex. If he was honest, everything about her—from her dazed expression to the way she used her hands when she talked and how that black suit conformed to her shape like a second skin—made him think of sex.

Sex and the promise of more. So much more.

Which was troubling. Because he'd been there, done that. The future before him with Kylie had been filled with such promise, such love and devotion. Then it had vanished in an instant, leaving him lost and alone. Brock never wanted to be eviscerated like that again. Promise and love and devotion didn't last, so it was better forgotten.

No matter how enticing the packaging might be.

And Cassie's present packaging was extremely enticing. Seeing her all polished up like a new penny had a way of messing with a guy's brain. Or maybe that was just him, since he hadn't been with a woman in so long that he'd nearly forgotten how it felt.

Nearly.

The pulse at the base of Cassie's slender neck—revealed by the unbuttoned, open neck of her white blouse—beat a little harder and faster than it should. Plus, his own heart raced too. Mostly because he couldn't seem to stop thinking about undoing the rest of those buttons and seeing what she had on underneath that suit.

Good God.

What he really needed was five minutes of solid sleep. And possibly a lobotomy. Or maybe to get laid.

But none of those things were likely to happen when he worked eighty-plus hours a week.

Blowing out a breath, Brock scooped up the puppy again—he suspected Riley had adopted Winnie for him and Adi with the sole purpose of sending her brother over the edge—and led Cassie back toward the house.

"I'm sorry I lost your dog," she said after grabbing her shoes and catching up to him.

Winnie perked up and licked Brock's face.

"It's so great you found her," Cassie added. "I was really worried there for a second."

"Yeah." Brock sighed in grim resignation, swiping puppy drool off his chin. "*So* great."

He had to get back to work. Dog tucked beneath his arm like a football, Brock headed for the front door, leaving Cassie standing by her SUV.

He'd just opened the door when Cassie called from behind him. "I'm so sorry for your loss. Kylie and your parents."

That stopped him cold. It had been years since anyone in town had mentioned them, allowing him to lock his feelings safely away. But, of course, Cassie hadn't been around in a while, so she'd brought it up again.

Lips compressed, Brock turned and leveled her with a long, assessing look. Why the hell did she have to come back now, dredging up the past? With her fancy clothes and her fancy hair and her fancy new attitude. He was bone-weary from working around the clock without sleep. He should've put the puppy away and went about his business. But instead, Brock found himself crossing back to where Cassie stood under the portico. "Why are you here?"

"I told you earlier. To see my dad and to consult on a case at the hospital." Then she smiled at Winnie, who soaked up the attention as her due. "And to walk your adorable dog."

Brock glanced down at Winnie, still tucked under his arm, because it was better than staring at Cassie, which did all sorts of naughty things inside him. "She's not *my* dog," he said. "Winnie belongs to my daughter, Adilyn. Gifted to her by Riley, who I'm pretty sure bought her from Satan."

Cassie chuckled, the sound sending a bolt of unwanted lust straight south for him. Jesus. He really needed to get that under control.

"Well, if you don't want her," she said. "Couldn't you just give her back?"

Now it was Brock's turn to laugh. "You don't have kids, I take it?"

"No."

"Trust me," he said. "I'm stuck with the dog."

"Arf!" Winnie agreed.

The air between them stretched taut again, filled with possibilities and all that promise.

Enough.

"Well, it was nice seeing you, Cassie." Brock shook his head and started toward his front door again, his long legs eating up the distance with ease. "Enjoy your time in Wyckford."

CHAPTER THREE

"THIS IS ALL your fault," Brock told a wriggling Winnie once they were safely inside.

The puppy didn't care. She'd already caught sight of her favorite squeaky toy and struggled maniacally to get free so she could attack.

Brock tightened his grip as he used his other hand to reach into his pocket for his phone, only to find his battery was dead. Seemed about right, given his day so far.

"You could have kept running for the hills," he told Winnie.

Winnie licked Brock's chin again.

"Yeah, yeah." His mind was still stuck on seeing Cassie, but he didn't have time to sleep, much less figure out the workings of that woman's mind.

Adi, who was five, had started kindergarten this week, so the house was currently void of craft kits and the beeps of his daughter's favorite Lola droid toy from that new show on Disney

Channel. She'd identified with a certain young galactic princess right away and now it was all Adi talked about these days. When she talked, that was.

And Riley was at the hospital. She'd returned to her job as a radiology tech at Wyckford General as soon as she could after the accident and routinely put in almost as many hours there as Brock did. They shared the house more for convenience than anything.

Moving through the kitchen, Brock secured Winnie back in her doggy prison, then refilled her food and water bowls. If he left it for his housekeeper, Lois, she'd quit for sure since she'd already made it clear nothing dog related was on her plate. And the last thing Brock needed was for yet another person to quit on him. It took a village to run his life, and his village always seemed to be in chaos these days. Everyone knew it too, because this was Wyckford. You could drop a million dollars on the pier and someone would hand it back to you, but you couldn't keep things secret to save your life.

Brock decided to change his scrubs while he was there, so he stripped in the laundry room and slid Winnie a long look. Unconcerned, the dog snuffled around in her bed, turning in circles before plopping down with a snort and closing her eyes, apparently satisfied with the destruction she'd left in her wake.

The house phone rang, probably because his cell wasn't charged. Brock grabbed a set of fresh scrubs from the delivered stack he kept in a basket on the dryer and headed for the door without answering the phone.

Whatever it was, he'd deal with it later.

This is how he survived the daily grind of his life—by prioritizing and organizing according to importance. Taking care of his family? Important. Incoming phone call to inform him he was late? Redundant, and therefore not critical.

Besides the four days a week Brock spent in his dad's practice, he also took two consult shifts in the ER. Weird, but even though his parents had died over four years ago now, Brock still didn't think of the GP office as his own, despite assuming all the responsibilities of running it. When he could, he also donated time to the local free clinic at the hospital. All the work kept him busy, but it was hell on his home life and his daughter.

Something had to give, and soon. Probably his sanity.

But for now, Brock headed back to the hospital only to be called into a board meeting.

The topic at hand didn't surprise him. The board wanted Brock to sell the practice so they could incorporate it into the hospital system as many of the other local medical practitioners had done. The deal they proposed was to buy him out, then pay him to stay on and hire on another doctor to help him with the workload. Plus, they'd guarantee the practice the hospital's internal referrals.

It wasn't the first time they'd made the offer either. In fact, they'd been after him all year to sell, each time getting more aggressive. But Brock didn't like being strong-armed, and he also didn't like thinking about how his dad would feel if Brock let the hard-earned practice slip from his control.

It was eight-thirty by the time he got home again that night—half an hour past Adi's bedtime. Last night, his daughter had been asleep at this time, legs curled under her with her butt in the air, her chubby baby face smashed into her pillow. She'd clearly gone to bed directly from the bath because her long, dark hair had stuck up all over, the same way Brock's did when his was wet and he didn't comb it. He'd knelt by her bed to stroke that perpetually unruly hair. Adi had stirred and...

Beeped.

As she'd done ever since Riley had brought home that sci-fi toy. His sister had assured him it was a passing phase.

Brock desperately hoped she was right.

His daughter was the spitting image of him, but she had her mother's imagination and temperament. Brock could read it in every line of his daughter's carefree body as she slept with wild abandon. He wondered if Kylie could see it too, from wherever she was now. But rationally he knew she couldn't, because to do so she'd have to see Adi, which she couldn't because she'd died.

Hoping that tonight his daughter might still be up—and perhaps using actual words—Brock walked in the front door and stopped in his tracks as Riley sped her wheelchair around the corner on two wheels. Hard to believe someone so petite could move so fast, but Brock knew better than to underestimate his twenty-nine-year-old sister.

She'd created a figure-eight racecourse between the two couches and the dining room table and was gaining serious speed. Seated in her lap, squealing, was Adi—not asleep, nowhere close. With her blue eyes lit with excitement, cheeks ruddy from exertion, his daughter smiled from ear to ear.

Winnie was right on their heels—or wheels, in this case—barking with wild delight, following as fast as her little legs would take her.

For a brief second, Brock stood rooted to the spot by a deep, undefined ache in his chest, which was replaced by terror an instant later as Riley took a corner far too tight. Her wheelchair wobbled, then tipped over, sending her and Adi flying.

Brock rushed over to the crumpled heap of limbs.

"Don't move," he ordered Riley, pulling Adi off her. He turned his daughter in his arms and cupped her face, so like his own, except for the exhaustion and cynicism dogging Brock's every breath. "You okay, sweetie?"

Adi grinned and threw her arms around her dad's neck in greeting. The kid's moods were pure and mercurial—another trait she'd inherited from her mother—but she loved with a fierceness that grabbed Brock by the throat. He hugged his daughter hard.

Letting out a breath, Brock set his daughter aside to lean over Riley, who hadn't moved. He knew better than to think she'd stayed still simply because he'd ordered her to, though. The only person who controlled his sister was Riley herself.

"Hey, sis." Gently Brock pushed the damp hair from her sweaty brow. "Talk to me."

Riley opened her eyes and laughed outright. "That was *fun*."

Adi tipped back her head and giggled, the sound filled with glee.

Brock sat on his heels and scrubbed a hand over his face. "Adi should be in bed. And you could have hurt yourself, Riley."

She started to crawl to her chair. "Been there, done that, bought the T-shirt."

Brock scooped her up, righted the wheelchair, then set his sister into it with a look of grumpy disapproval.

"Oh, relax," Riley muttered as Brock stood over her, hands on hips. She tugged on Adi's ear. "Hey, sweetie pie. Go get ready for bed."

"Beep beep," Adi said, then turned to the hallway.

Brock called after his daughter. "Use toothpaste tonight."

Adi scrunched her nose and scratched her head.

But Brock had learned never to cave. "Go on. I'll be right there."

Adi went from bummed to excited in a single heartbeat, because if her dad was coming too, it meant a story. And for a moment, Brock's chest ached again. Getting home in time to fall into bed exhausted was one thing. Getting home in time to spend a few minutes with his daughter before they both crashed was even better.

"Pick out a book," he said.

"Beep!"

Riley ignored Brock and pushed back her

dark hair before wheeling away. She was petite, but not frail. Never frail. She had the haunting beauty of a fairytale princess and the fortitude of a warrior.

The same car accident that had killed their parents had left Riley a highly functioning paraplegic. She was lucky to be alive, though it'd been hard at first to convince his sister of that fact. Now, Riley didn't accept anyone's pity, and she certainly didn't need anyone's help. Stubbornness. Another family trait they shared.

"If you can't get Adi to bed on time," Brock said as his sister rolled away, "I'll come home and do it myself."

"Please do." Riley wheeled back around to face him, making a show of looking behind him. "Oh, good. Glad to see you still have the stick up your ass, bro." Then she headed into the foyer, grabbing her purse off the bench. "I'm going out. Don't wait up."

"Riley, c'mon." Brock's fingers curled helplessly. Riley living here worked out well for them. Sometimes. Like when Brock needed a sitter for Adi and Riley wasn't working. Other times, not so much. Like now. "It's late. Where are you going?"

"A place called none of your business." Riley threw her hands up in the air. "I'll see you later."

"Wake me up when you get home."

She rolled her eyes and left. Brock waited until she was safely ensconced in her specially appointed vehicle and drove off before he shut the door.

Unfortunately, he knew she'd been struggling since getting out of rehab as she tried to adjust to all the changes in her life. Hell, he'd been the same after Kylie's death. Then the accident that had taken their parents and put Riley in the ICU for weeks had taken away the last of his support system. When his sister had been released from the rehabilitation hospital after three months, Brock had become solely responsible for a badly injured, headstrong, angry Riley along with his infant daughter. He'd held it together, barely, but it'd all been a hell of an adjustment, and there'd been more than a few times Brock hadn't been sure he was going to make it.

Sometimes he still wasn't sure.

He locked up, set the alarm, flipped off the lights in the kitchen and living room, then found Adi jumping on her bed with her stuffed bear.

Brock caught his daughter around the waist midleap, tossed her onto the bed and then crawled in after her.

Adi had a few books picked out for him to choose from. Being read to calmed Adi, and she snuggled up close, resting her head on Brock's shoulder as she pointed to the top book on the stack—*Family Is Everything*. The cover showed the characters on the cover, but Adi's finger went right to the mother.

The significance wasn't lost on Brock and felt like a knife to his heart. "Adi."

She tucked her face into his chest, but Brock gently palmed his daughter's head and pulled her back enough to see her face. "You remember what I told you, right? About your mom? She's here with you, even if you can't see her. In your heart."

Adi stared at him, her blue eyes huge as she nodded.

And for the umpteenth time in the past five years, Brock wanted to curse Buzzards Bay. For taking his wife. For taking Adi's mother. For taking everything from him. But it didn't do any good. So, instead, he pressed a kiss to Adi's forehead and sighed. "Should we start the story?"

He woke somewhere near dawn, dreaming he couldn't breathe. When Brock opened his eyes, he realized he'd fallen asleep in Adi's bed. His daughter had one half of the twin mattress, Winnie the other, both blissfully sleeping, limbs and paws akimbo.

And Brock, bigger than them both combined times four, had one tiny little corner of space. His feet were numb from hanging off, and the book they'd been reading was stuck to his face. Wincing at his stiff joints, he shifted, then eased out of the bed, pulling the covers up over a still-sleeping Adi.

Envying her, Brock showered and went downstairs.

Lois was cleaning the kitchen and making Adi's lunch.

"I need you to walk Winnie today," Brock said. "Twice. Once midmorning and once in the afternoon."

Lois carefully closed Adi's lunch box. "No."

His housekeeper was four and a half feet tall, Italian—complete with an accent—and snapping black eyes that could slay one alive. Lois also possessed the baffling ability to organize Brock's home so it looked like humans lived there instead of a pack of wild animals. But she didn't cook, and she didn't mother. The sole reason the woman made his daughter's lunch was because Adi was the only one in the house Lois actually liked.

"I do not care for *that* dog," she said. "It licks me."

"Winnie's a puppy," Brock said. "That's what they do."

"It's a nightmare."

Well, she had him there.

CHAPTER FOUR

HALF AN HOUR LATER, Brock had gotten Adi onto the school bus, then driven to the office, still having no idea what he was going to do about the dog.

He could call Cassie, but that would involve being sucked into her sexy vortex again. Plus, he had no idea what her plans were back here in Wyckford. She'd mentioned seeing her dad and her friends, and something about consulting on a case, but none of that involved walking his dog. With a sigh, Brock scrolled through all his contacts and couldn't find one who'd be available to help him on such short notice.

Brock stared out his office window, wondering what case Cassie was consulting on.

Her specialty was plastic and reconstructive surgery. Given the size of Wyckford, it was most likely a patient Brock knew and had worked on himself. If—and that was a major "if"—he asked her to walk Winnie again, it would give him a chance to find out more. Strictly professional, of course. So, against his better judgement, he hit redial on the number he'd called from the flyer yesterday. The call rang and rang, then finally went to voice mail, meaning Cassie was busy or screening his calls. Considering their less than stellar reunion, he'd bet good money on the latter.

Out of options, he left his car and headed to his practice, by way of the old west wing of Wyckford General Hospital, where the free clinic was located.

Madison Scott, the nurse who ran it, smiled when he entered. "Hey, Doc. Tell me you're here to give me a shift."

"No, why? You need someone?"

"The doctor who was scheduled for today ended up with an emergency in Boston and can't show."

Brock eyed the full waiting room. "Not sure what I have waiting for me in the office, but I'll try to get back over here later if I can."

"Thanks," she said gratefully. "But if you're not here to work, what can I do for you?"

"I wondered if you knew where Cassie Murphy might be."

Madi arched a brow at him, her expression curious. "Why are you looking for her? Another dog-walking emergency?"

Brock grimaced. He'd hoped Cassie wouldn't spread that news around, but he should've known better. Cassie and Madi were good friends. Of course they'd talk about it. Jesus, he didn't have time for this. Neither of them did, based on that busy waiting room. He tried again. "Do you know where I might find her?"

Madi sighed. "She mentioned going to see her father today at Sunny Village."

"Thanks." Brock moved to the door, then turned back to Madi. "Can you call my staff and tell them I'm running half an hour behind, please?"

"It'll cost you."

"Let me guess," Brock said. "Chocolate cake?"

The nurse smiled sweetly. "From the Buzzy Bird, please."

"Noted." Brock left the free clinic and drove through Wyckford, past the town pier, to the area's only retirement home. Sunny Village occupied an old Victorian mansion, possessing over a century's worth of charm and character as it sat comfortably on its foundation in its old age. When he stepped inside, a bell above his head chimed, and Ben Murphy, Cassie's dad, poked his head out of a room down the hall.

Close to eighty, he had the craggy, weather-beaten features of seafarers everywhere and wore khakis and a plaid shirt. As a lifelong resident of Wyckford, the man was the heart and soul of the community—not to mention a major hub for all things gossip. "Dr. Turner!" Ben beamed at the sight of him, coming down the hall to greet Brock. "Are you here to join our drawing class?"

"No, I came looking for your daughter. Is Cassie here?"

Ben blinked. "Yep, she is. In the art studio, filling in as our model today."

Not much surprised Brock, but this did. He couldn't imagine shy, mousy Cassie voluntarily standing in front of anyone. But then, based on yesterday, Cassie was neither shy, nor mousy any longer. Images of her with long, flowing hair and not much else on, flooded his mind before he could stop himself. Dammit. Brock cleared his throat and tried again. "She's modeling for your art class?"

"We're learning to sketch the human form. Standard practice for beginners," Ben said. "Our regular model didn't show, and since Cassie was already here to see me, I asked if she minded doing it."

Ben led him down the hall and pushed the studio door open, revealing Cassie on a dais—fully clothed, thank goodness—wearing a formfitting black top and pants, her body twisted into a ballerina pose. Her long hair hung loose down her back in waves, shining like silk, her limbs lithe and graceful.

Ben grinned. "She's doing a great job."

Still holding her position, Cassie narrowed her gaze on Brock. "Why are you here?"

"He came to see you," her father called.

The whole situation should've been ridiculous, but it wasn't. Not at all. In fact, Cassie looked good enough to gobble up with a spoon. Or his tongue would work too…

"Why are you here?" Cassie asked him again, her tone chilly.

"Winnie needs a walker today. I thought you might be available."

Without saying a word or moving a muscle, she managed to say no. It was all in the gaze.

Man, he'd never realized how amazing Cassie's eyes were.

"Honey, you're looking a little tense," Ben said to his daughter. "Can you go back to tranquil?"

She did, and Brock bowed his head and studied his shoes. It wasn't often he felt unsure, but he had no idea what to do with Cassie Murphy back in town. Honestly, he leave the woman alone. He had no time for this. None. And yet, he couldn't. Worrisome, that.

"Look," she said to him from up on the dais. "I nearly lost your dog yesterday. Why would you want me back? I'm a terrible walker. Find someone else. I'll stick with medicine, thanks."

"You weren't terrible."

"You're just saying that so I'll help you out."

Well, yeah. He was. But he was also in a real bind. "Please?"

All the residents in the room were following their conversation like it was a tennis match, and all eyes had landed on Cassie now. The audience waited breathlessly for her answer.

"I really don't think that's a good idea, Dr. Turner," she finally said. "Sorry."

In unison, the heads swiveled back to Brock.

So, they were back to last names again. Perfect. He drew a breath and tried again. "Look. I'm sorry too, Dr. Murphy. It was all a misunderstanding. Yesterday I was overworked, stressed and in a hurry. Can we try again? As colleagues this time?"

This got Cassie's attention enough to make her break the pose. Hell, it got *everyone's* attention.

Even Ben set down his pencil. "What do you think?" he asked the room of mainly blue-haired ladies. "Should my daughter walk Dr. Turner's dog?"

They whispered among themselves like jurors

debating a sentence as Brock slid Cassie a look. She stared back at him, her hazel eyes now lit with amusement.

"Six to two," Ben announced, "in favor of my Cassie giving Brock another shot."

At first, Cassie didn't react at all, and he feared the worst. Then she smiled. And man. She'd always had a great smile. Something inside Brock twinged then, something he'd thought dead. He dug the toe of his loafer into the beige carpet. "Seems the people have spoken."

Cassie stepped down off the dais and walked over to him, her wary hazel eyes warning him that he was on thin ice, but Brock had no clue what he'd done now. "Guess they have."

"Break time, class!" Ben clapped his hands, then slid a sly look in Brock's direction and whispered, "Don't blow it."

Cassie stood about a foot away, her mouth curving into a smile, slow and sensuous. "Are you sure this is a good idea?"

No. No, he wasn't sure at all. But for some reason, instead of calling the whole thing off, Brock stepped close to Cassie, his gaze searching hers for a sign.

Her smile broadened.

"You're the only option I have," he said softly, narrowing his eyes.

"How flattering."

She was taunting him, and he liked it. Another danger sign. He had too many people to worry about already. Cassie would be out of the picture soon, out of his life for good. Which meant bringing her into his daughter's orbit was impossible. The last thing he wanted was for Adi to become attached to Cassie and then have her leave.

Maybe she doesn't have to meet your daughter, though...

That last thought stopped him short, drew him closer. Meaning what? They could have an affair. A no-strings fling? Interesting. And a little bit of a turn-on if he was honest.

Infuriating. Since the only thing he was certain of where Cassie was concerned was that she was a brilliant doctor and a horrible dog walker. She could be married, engaged, any number of other possibilities that would put her squarely beyond Brock's reach.

But screw it. He was tired of thinking. So, instead, he leaned in and brushed his mouth over hers. Why? He couldn't say exactly, other than maybe exhaustion. And need. And wanting to know if those lips of hers tasted as good as they looked. Seemingly as shocked by his actions as he was, Cassie stiffened beneath him. Peach.

Her mouth tasted like peaches—more delicious than anything he could remember.

So was the kiss, chaste as it was, which rocked his socks right off.

CHAPTER FIVE

CASSIE'S EYES OPENED wide in shock when Brock Turner kissed her. Then, slowly, they slid closed as she enjoyed the feel of his lips on hers. And yep, they were every bit as heavenly as she'd always imagined they would be. Maybe even more so. There were sparks too, at least for her.

Or more like a full fireworks display.

When Brock pulled back, Cassie opened her eyes again to his bright blue ones and caught a hint of surprise in his gaze before he masked it.

"So you'll walk my dog today then?" he asked, a bit gruffer than before.

For the first time since he'd arrived, Cassie noticed he looked even more exhausted than he had yesterday. She was also extremely aware of his proximity after their unexpected kiss, aware of the cargo pants and button-down shirt he wore, both in black, both casual but expensive looking, like he'd walked right out of an ad.

Aware that the entire art class was still watching them from the doorway, including her dad.

Great.

Cassie stepped back and crossed her arms. "Fine. I'll walk Winnie."

Brock handed her a key to his house and told her the code for the alarm then left.

"Hey," she called, running to catch up with him in the hall, her body still humming. "Wait. What was that in there?"

"You know what it was."

Yeah, Cassie knew all right. Chemistry. But why did it have to happen now? With this man? She'd spent years forgetting him and with one kiss Brock threatened to wipe out all her hard work. Not to mention they were night and day. Oil and water. No. That kiss had to have been a fluke. A crazy one-off, never to be repeated.

Then Brock's eyes darkened, and her pulse tripped in response.

Okay, maybe not a fluke then.

Cassie hazarded a glance over her shoulder and found her dad and the entire art class still there by the door, eavesdropping. She scowled and waved them away, and they vanished.

"Impressive." Brock snorted. "Be sure to use that level of authority on Winnie today and try to avoid another escape."

"I really thought she'd drowned."

"She likes to play hide-and-seek."

"Good to know."

He took a deep breath, then rocked back on his heels. "Who's your patient?"

"I'm sorry?" Cassie frowned.

"The one you're consulting on here. You mentioned it yesterday."

"Oh. Right." Cassie nodded. "Her name is Serene Ogden."

"I know Serene," Brock said. "I worked on her initially when she came into the ER after her accident. Did her initial surgery to stabilize her enough to get her to this point. I can go over the records with you if you'd like. I'll have my office set it up."

He smiled then—a genuine one, from a man who she suspected didn't do so very often anymore—and it left Cassie a little dazed. Or maybe it was the residual buzz left over from their kiss. Whatever the cause, she found herself nodding against her better judgment. "I'd like that."

"Great." He continued toward the exit, calling to her as he went. "Let me know if you have any trouble with Winnie. The house should be empty again, just like before."

"We'll be fine," she called back. And she would be too. Just as soon as she got over the fact she and Brock had a connection, a real one, and now she knew the power of it.

Except she wasn't back home to make connections. Not with Brock Turner anyway. She was here to see her dad and her friends and consult on Serene's case. Then she was going back to San Diego and her life there. Which meant steering well clear of anything beyond the professional was her smartest choice. And no matter how good Brock and his kisses were, she was going to be smart if it killed her.

A few hours later, Cassie let herself into Brock's house without incident. This time, she carefully leashed the dog *before* opening the baby gate and, as a double precaution, she carefully picked up Winnie and carried her outside.

They avoided the beach entirely, instead walking along the sidewalk down the quiet street. The puppy sniffed every single rock and tree, then finally chose a spot to do her business.

Afterward, Cassie took Winnie back to the house and secured her in the laundry room before grabbing her bag to leave. But as she turned to the door, she found that they weren't alone anymore. Riley in her wheelchair filled the doorway.

"Hey," Riley said. They hugged. "You look great, Cassie. I wouldn't have recognized you if I hadn't seen the picture."

Cassie frowned. "What picture?"

"This one." Riley pulled out her phone and

thumbed a few buttons, then turned the screen toward Cassie.

Her heart dropped. Front and center on Wyckford's Facebook page was a photo of Cassie and Brock from the retirement home earlier. And even though the kiss had lasted only a heartbeat, the image had been captured at just the right second, with Cassie leaning into Brock with both hands on his chest. And Brock was cupping her jaw, his thumb stroking her skin in a way that seemed both tender and yet, somehow, outrageously sexy.

She hadn't realized they'd done that at the time, but now Cassie remembered Brock's body heat radiating against her palms and the easy strength of his body. And he'd smelled delicious. Like sandalwood and spice.

"Cozy," Riley said, jarring Cassie from her thoughts.

"It's not what it looks like." Cassie handed the phone back.

"No?" Riley looked at the screen again. "Because it looks like you're kissing my brother."

"Okay. Yes, we're kissing, but that's only because…" Cassie trailed off, unable to remember exactly how she'd ended up with Brock's mouth on hers. On the internet.

Riley arched a brow. "Because why?"

Cassie sighed. "We're not… I mean, he and I aren't—"

"No worries." Riley tapped her screen a few times before putting her phone away in her pocket. "There. Just had to share the link with everyone in town. I love it when my brother does something stupid. It's so rare. But when he finally does it, he really does it right."

She grinned and unlocked the baby gate, freeing Winnie just as a young girl burst into the kitchen from the open doorway. She waved around what looked like a small flying saucer as she ran circles around the kitchen table.

Winnie nipped at the girl's heels and barked so hard her front legs came off the floor.

The girl wore jeans and a pink T-shirt with a cartoon figure holding two beakers filled with glitter and the word "Science" in block letters across the top. Her pink sneakers lit up with each step and the left one was untied. She looked maybe five, with long dark hair that hadn't seen a brush since morning, and the same bright blue eyes as Brock's. The little girl stopped short at the sight of Cassie, and Winnie plowed into the back of her, then yelped.

"Adi, sweetie," Riley said. "This is Cassie. She's a friend of your dad's and mine. She's going to watch you for an hour or so while I run some errands, okay?"

Those words took a second to register in Cassie's brain, but when they did, she protested. "Wait…what? No, I'm just here to walk the dog."

But Riley was already gone, the door closing behind her.

Crap.

When Cassie turned back to the kitchen and little Adi, she found Winnie chewing on the kitchen table leg. "Hey," she scolded the puppy. "Don't do that. Bad doggy."

Winnie kept chewing. Cassie went over and pried the puppy loose, but she was too late. There were deep gouges in the beautiful wood.

The girl watched her, solemn faced, those blue eyes giving nothing away.

"Hi," Cassie said, putting the dog back behind the gate and then crouching in front of Brock's daughter.

It was going to be a long hour.

Cassie straightened and searched for some way to entertain a five-year-old kid who held a UFO. "Do you like space?"

Adi swung her toy wide. It lit up and beeped.

The dog promptly went nuts, so naturally Adi swung it again.

The toy clipped a cup of juice on the kitchen table, sending it flying. Luckily it was plastic. Not so luckily, the juice inside it was grape. Purple sticky liquid splattered all over the table, the floor and the counters. Cassie, Winnie and Adi too. Even the ceiling took a hit.

Adi dropped her UFO as if it were a hot potato, her eyes welling with tears.

The dog barked nonstop now.

"It's okay," Cassie said to a stricken Adi, grabbing a roll of paper towels from the counter to clean up the kid first. But the sticky clothes didn't appear to bother the little girl because as soon as Cassie let her go, she headed toward the fridge.

Winnie redirected her energy to licking the drops of grape juice that had made it as far as the laundry room floor.

"Adi?" Cassie asked. "Where's the trash?"

The girl made a vague gesture toward the back door, then stuck her head into the fridge.

Cassie wiped down the kitchen, then stepped outside with a wad of sticky paper towels, which she dumped into the trash can she found there. Now that she had a moment of privacy, she pulled out her cell phone and hit Brock's number to fill him in on the new developments.

He picked up, sounding harried. "Dr. Turner."

Her brain stuttered at the sound of his low voice, the same low voice that had prompted her into a moment of insanity earlier. And, of course, their kiss...

That kiss.

"It's Cassie." She tried for calm efficiency with her tone. She was known for her calm efficiency, after all. Order. Balance. Or she *had* been before she'd returned to Wyckford.

Cassie turned the knob on the back door to return to the kitchen and…nothing.

It was locked. And her key was in her bag inside.

"What's wrong?" Brock asked.

"Uh…nothing." Cassie peered into the window, thankful the shades were open, but didn't see Adi in the kitchen. "Well, nothing except, just as I was getting ready to leave, your sister and your daughter arrived. Riley had an errand, so she left Adi here with me to watch until she gets back."

There was another beat of silence while Brock apparently processed this, then he said tightly, "Riley left you with Adi?"

"She did."

Nothing about her answer seemed to please Brock. But before Cassie could think too long on why that was, she remembered their photo gracing the top of the town's social media page. She'd intended on breaking that news to him as well but decided it could wait until later. Or never. Seeing as how he didn't seem to be in the best mood.

"Don't worry. We'll be fine," Cassie said, as

much for Brock as herself. "It should only be for an hour."

She tried the door again. Still locked. She knocked.

Winnie panted and barked from behind the gate in the laundry room, but still no sign of the kid. She knocked again. "Adi?"

The dog froze, then turned toward a basket of scrubs in the laundry room. Winnie started nosing around it. The container wobbled but didn't tip. Then the puppy sank her teeth into the plastic liner and tugged until the thing fell over, spilling scrubs across the floor. *Not good.*

Cassie looked around. She was in a side yard with two gates—one at either end. She tried both. Both were locked. "I have to go."

"Don't even think about it. What's wrong?"

Oh, so many, *many* things. Through the window, Cassie saw Winnie going to town on a pair of scrub pants. Adi was still nowhere in sight. Cassie knocked again, harder this time.

Winnie looked up and growled.

Cassie whirled around, searching for where a spare key might be hidden. Everyone had one for emergencies, right? Except there were no pots or mat to hide one under near the door. Most likely because it was safer for Riley in her wheelchair that way. Made sense.

"Cassie. Where is my daughter?"

She took another peek in the window and, thank God, the little girl now stood on the other side of the door, staring up at her with those big blue eyes. Cassie pointed to the door handle.

Adi just looked at her.

"She's in the kitchen." Cassie sighed and closed her eyes, rubbing a finger between her brows. Best to put it all out there since she wasn't making much progress on her own. "And I'm locked out. Do you keep a spare key?"

"Second planter from the porch," Brock instructed, that slight edge still in his tone. Anger, apprehension, supreme annoyance? Probably all three, considering he now knew Adi was with the same person who'd lost his dog the day before. "It's in the sprinkler valve box."

Holding the phone in the crook of her neck, Cassie gave the little girl what she hoped was a reassuring smile and pointed to the door handle once more, gesturing for Adi to let her in.

Instead, the kid walked out of the kitchen for parts unknown, her shoelace trailing behind her.

"Adi!" Cassie called. "Adi, don't leave the kitchen. *Adilyn?*"

"Hurry!" Brock said in her ear, urgency overriding the worry in his tone. "Do you see it?"

Cassie rushed to the second planter and yeah, she saw it. She also saw a big, hairy brown spider guarding its web that covered the sprinkler box.

"Cassie," Brock said, sounding every inch the cool, calm, trauma surgeon she knew him to be in the ER. "There's a pool out back. You can't get to it from the side yard where you are. Adi can swim, but…"

Oh, God.

The thought of his daughter drowning was too awful to bear. No. He'd lost too much already. Cassie refused to hurt him anymore. So, eyes closed, she plunged her hand through the web and pulled out the Hide-a-Key. Then she ran back to the door and let herself in, raced through the kitchen and skidded to a halt in the living room, where Adi stood on the couch, toy once again in hand, whipping it around.

Cassie nearly collapsed with relief. She'd handled some of the most difficult and delicate reconstructive surgeries in the world without breaking a sweat, yet after one hour with this little girl and a dog, she needed a nap. "Well, that was a fun fire drill."

"My daughter?" Brock asked in Cassie's ear. "Is she okay?"

"Yes. She's fine." She sank onto the couch and

took a deep breath. "My nerves, on the other hand… Your house is crazy, Dr. Turner."

"Did you lose Winnie?"

"No."

"Then you're already doing better than yesterday," he said. He mumbled something offline that she didn't catch, then said, "I'll get there as soon as I can."

"But—"

Brock ended the call. Cassie lifted her head and found Adi watching her, dark hair falling across the little girl's forehead, toy still in one hand, and a squirming Winnie in the other. She must've gotten the dog out of the laundry room.

They were both adorable. And this would be okay. Cassie had graduated medical school at the top of her class. She could totally handle one five-year-old and a puppy for an hour. It was sort of like wrangling all the partners at their weekly meetings for the plastic surgery practice.

Then Adi wrinkled her nose like something was stinky and hastily set the dog down where Winnie promptly vomited.

That had never happened at one of the partner meetings.

Winnie then fell asleep, apparently feeling all better.

"Beep," Adi said.

CHAPTER SIX

ONE PAINFULLY LONG hour later, Cassie was exhausted.

The dog had found a forgotten blood pressure cuff from somewhere and had dragged it through the living room—around the couch, up and over the coffee table—until it had gotten trapped around a chair leg. Then a sound like a leaking balloon had come from Winnie, and she'd fallen over, legs straight up in the air.

Cassie thought the puppy had killed herself again. But nope. Winnie had rebounded.

Five minutes later, she was chewing on her toys.

And the wooden kitchen chairs.

And the wooden banister poles.

And someone's forgotten mittens...

Finally, the front door opened. Brock stepped inside, wearing a white lab coat over his office clothes and a stethoscope around his neck. He picked up Adi and put her over his shoulder in a fireman's hold, making the kid squeal with delight.

Those stress lines around Brock's eyes and mouth were deeper now as he turned to Cassie, his daughter still hanging upside down. "Riley?"

"I'm here," his sister called, rolling through the door behind him. "Sorry. Had to run back to the hospital to finish up some things."

"Why didn't you call me if Adi was ready to be picked up?" Brock asked his sister. "You know I don't…"

Riley winced. "Sorry. I got the call from her school while I was in the middle of a set of films and one of the techs took over for me so I could leave and get her and…" Brock's sister sighed and shook her head. "I should have called. But I thought it was a simple thing and I'd be helping you out." She headed for the hallway. "Excuse me for trying to make things easier on you, bro."

A few moments later a door closed—to Riley's room, Cassie supposed.

She and Brock stared at each other for a couple of long, uncomfortable beats before he finally said, "Thanks."

"It was no problem, really," she said, pushing to her feet, then fidgeting slightly. "I mean, after I got back in the house and all."

"Listen, about my daughter…" Brock started before Cassie cut him off.

"She's a very sweet kid." Cassie hurried back to the kitchen to get her bag. "But I think I've got a long way to go before I win any babysitting awards." She gave a small chuckle to cover her anxiety. She'd always thought she'd make an okay mom someday, even though she hadn't had one herself. But after today, Cassie wasn't so sure. Still, now was not the time or the place. "I'll stick to what I know. Medicine and surgery."

"Cassie." Brock sighed and put Adi down, then reached into his pocket for his wallet. "At least let me—"

"No. Seriously. Don't worry about it. It's fine."

From across the room, he gave her a speculative gaze and her tummy quivered.

Cassie laughed it off as best she could. "Honestly. I came to walk Winnie and ended up staying a bit longer to do more. It's no problem. Really. Saved me from modeling at the retirement home again. I should be thanking you."

His gaze flicked to her lips, and her whole body tingled. "I owe you one then."

The air between them seemed to do that whole snap-crackle-pop thing, like static electricity on steroids, and Cassie's breath caught as she backed toward the door. Softly, she said, "Okay. You owe me one."

* * *

Thanks to another crazy shift in the ER, Brock didn't get home again that night until 3:00 a.m. He crawled into bed and immediately crashed, dreaming about a certain beautiful plastic surgeon in a black outfit that clung to her curves and made his heart pound.

And thanks to his own stupidity, he also dreamed about kissing said beautiful surgeon.

He'd not planned on Cassie meeting his daughter. Not today. Not ever. Poor Adi had been through enough in her short life and the last thing Brock wanted was for her to lose someone else. It's why he never brought any of the women he slept with home. Why he hadn't dated anyone seriously since Kylie had died. He was a single father. That came with responsibilities. Ones he took very seriously. It made no sense to let someone into his home, into his life, into his daughter's life, if it wasn't going to last.

And with Cassie going back to California soon, there was no potential for forever.

No matter what his thudding heart might say.

He managed to get one glorious hour of sleep before Riley woke him up as she got ready for an early shift at the hospital.

When he finally got to his office, he found he'd been double booked, but that was nothing new either. First up was Mrs. Dupree, who com-

plained of hot flashes and other signs of peri-
menopause. She'd been coming in once a week
for months, bringing Brock casseroles along
with her list of symptoms. At the end of each
appointment, she asked him out. Each time, he
politely turned her down, saying he never mixed
business with pleasure. Today when he gave her
the standard line, she showed him a Facebook
pic…of him and Cassie kissing on her phone.

"Looks like definite mixing there, Doc," she
said.

Brock stared at the picture, a little surprised
to find that their crazy chemistry had absolutely
translated to the screen for the world to see. It
felt like the temperature in the exam room went
up by several degrees. "She's not my patient."

"No. She's a fellow doctor. And I have it on
good authority she walks your dog for you."

No use in getting annoyed about the gossip.
This was Wyckford, after all. He rose, pulled off
his gloves and tossed them into the trash bin,
giving his patient a bland smile. "See you next
week, Mrs. Dupree."

Mrs. Dupree harumphed.

Brock walked to the next patient room and
pulled the chart from the door holder. Mr. Stanley had kidney stones. Brock entered the room
and pulled on yet another set of gloves. He'd
once wondered how many hours a year he spent

pulling on and tearing off gloves and figured he didn't really want to know. "How are you doing today, Mr. Stanley?"

"I'm dying."

"Nope. You're not." Brock studied the man's test results and labs once more to make sure he wasn't missing anything. "It's kidney stones. And fortunately, they're small enough not to require surgery. Once they pass, you'll feel better."

"You sure?" the patient asked, grimacing.

"Yes."

"Really sure?" Mr. Stanley asked, not sounding convinced. "Because last night I felt like I was peeing fire."

"Just force liquids, and I'll prescribe you a little stronger pain medication to help, okay? And be sure to use the strainer we gave you when you urinate so we can collect the stones for the lab."

And so his day went, one patient after another until, by noon, his head was ready to explode, and he knew he couldn't go on like this. He either had to start turning patients away or give up the ER shifts.

"It's a no-brainer," Mark said at lunchtime. He'd brought deli club sandwiches from the place next to the fire station. They were spread out in Brock's office as they watched ESPN highlights on the computer. "Sell the practice to the hospital. Let them bring in another doc and all your problems go away. You work the hours you want."

Nothing was ever that simple, but the appeal was growing. It meant giving up his dad's dream, which he hated, but the truth was that Brock couldn't do the dream justice. He'd tried.

When Mark had gone back to work, Brock brought up the contract offer, which he'd read a hundred times. He'd had his attorney go over it with a fine-tooth comb. All he had to do was accept the offer with an electronic signature and hit the send button.

His finger hovered over the enter key, but then he set his head down on his desk to think about it for a minute. Next thing he knew, Darlene, his nurse practitioner, called his name.

"Hey," she grumbled from the doorway. "If you get to nap, so do I."

Darlene was in her fifties and the perfect mix of no-nonsense and sweet empathy for his patients, though she rarely felt the need to impart any of that sweet empathy on Brock.

"Need you to get your cute butt out here, Doc," she said. "You've got Nancy Kessler in room one with a UTI she wants cleared up before she goes to Vegas this weekend with her new boyfriend. Randy Lyons is in room two. He nail-gunned his thumb to the wall again. And

Mrs. Munson's in three, saying the high pollen count is going to kill her."

"You take the allergies," he said. "I'll get the other two."

"Here." Darlene handed him her coffee. "You probably need it more than I do."

"Thanks." It had far too much sugar and milk in it, but she was right. He needed it bad.

"Your father was never this busy," Darlene said.

"Because we've doubled his practice."

"*You* doubled his practice." She patted Brock's arm. "He'd be proud, but you need help, Brock. Before you burn out."

"I'm not going to burn out."

"Okay, then either sign the contract or get another doc in here before *I* burn out." With that, Darlene nabbed back her coffee and left.

Brock's other office staff members consisted of two front office clerks, Monica and Sherry, and an LPN named Coco. An hour later, Monica poked her head into the exam room. "Mrs. Preston on line two. Needs to see you today."

Mrs. Preston didn't need to see him. She was lonely. Her kids lived out in Oregon, so she came in at least once a week for attention. Last week she'd had an eye twitch and had self-diagnosed a brain tumor. "Tell her we can get her in tomorrow."

"She says tomorrow's too late."

"All right, fine. Squeeze her in today, then."

An hour later, the waiting room was still full. Darlene gave Brock the stink eye when he slipped into his office to take an incoming call from Adi's school.

His daughter hadn't been picked up by the nanny again.

Brock immediately headed for the door, giving Darlene an apologetic wave. He got into his car while dialing the nanny. She was the sister of one of the nurses at the hospital and had come highly recommended. Problem was, she was only a temporary fix because as soon as her husband's transfer came through, they were moving. He'd had three nannies this year alone.

Brock sensed a pattern, and he didn't have time for it.

The new nanny picked up and immediately said, "Don't hate me but I'm getting on a plane."

He let out a breath. "No notice?"

"I'm sorry. Everything happened much faster than expected."

Wasn't that the truth?

Brock considered thunking his head against his steering wheel.

He called his sister next, then remembered she was working and ended the call. Brock pictured Adi waiting at school with no one there, and his stomach cramped. He sped up while mentally thumbing through the contacts on his phone, slowing at Cassie's name.

Don't do it.

Cassie was a fantastic doctor, but she'd come through for him twice now during her brief return to Wyckford, *and that* was twice too much. No way should he burden her with this again. Except she'd already handled Adi yesterday for an hour, and the truth was, Cassie had already proven more reliable than half the people in his life. And there was something in her eyes that pulled him in like the tide, something unforgettable.

Which made this whole situation even more dangerous. Because not only was Brock falling under her spell, pretty soon his daughter might as well. Adi and Cassie had spent time together already the day before, and that should've been more than enough for Brock to put on the brakes where the two of them were concerned.

But he honestly didn't have anyone else. Even Lois had gone home to Italy to visit her family for a few weeks, leaving him zero options. He couldn't take Adi to work either. The last time he'd done that, she'd escaped his office and run amok in the waiting room, creating pandemonium. Things were chaotic enough today without a five-year-old tornado blowing through. So yeah. What other choice did he have?

Reluctantly, he hit Cassie's number and then waited. He'd talk to her, tell her the rules: Be friendly, but remote with his daughter. Don't form any lasting bonds.

Don't break my daughter's heart.

Cassie answered on the third ring. "Hello?"

"What are you doing right now?" Brock asked, more abruptly than he should have, but he was desperate.

"I just got back from walking Winnie. And don't listen to what your neighbors say about me. It isn't true. Mostly."

Confused by the direction this conversation was headed, Brock frowned. "Mostly?"

"Winnie defiled Mrs. Perry's petunias. Twice."

Exasperated, he waved it off. "Forget Mrs. Perry. I hate to do this, but I need another favor." Brock hesitated. His gut screamed no, but there really was no other choice. "Can you watch Adi again this afternoon for an hour or two while I finish at the office?"

Cassie went quiet, and Brock didn't want to rush her, but he had patients waiting—and Adi, who was hopefully not alone at the school Brock was still five blocks from.

Finally, she sighed and said, "Okay. But this really can't become a habit."

Brock let out a breath of relief. He couldn't agree more. "We'll be at the house shortly. Thanks, Cassie."

"Yeah, you probably shouldn't thank me yet."

He laughed softly, and there was another beat of their crazy chemistry through the phone.

Brock ended the call and pulled up to the school. His daughter stood on the curb, one hand in her teacher aide's, the other clutching her lunch box to her chest. He got out of the car and crouched in front of Adi. "Hey, sweetie. Sorry the nanny wasn't here to get you. She's moving a little sooner than expected."

Adi nodded and studied the tops of her sneakers.

Brock met the woman's gaze, and she gave him a look that screamed, *Epic fail, Dad.*

Message received, condescending teacher aide.

"Appreciate you waiting with her."

"It's my job," the aide said. "Adi pulled another vanishing act on us today."

"I didn't get a call."

"Because we found her. Thirty feet up the big oak tree in the playground."

Little black dots floated in Brock's visual field. As a trauma surgeon, he'd seen exactly what a thirty-foot fall could do to a body. He'd seen everything. Throat tight, he asked Adi, "What were you doing up there, sweetie?"

His daughter didn't respond, so the aide answered instead. "She had a tree frog clenched in one fist."

"She doesn't have a frog."

"No. But we do. Liberated from its terrarium in the kindergarten classroom."

Ah. Now it made sense. Brock looked at his daughter again. "You saved the frog, huh?"

Adi nodded.

"Oh, and she spoke today," the aide added.

"What did you say?" Brock asked his daughter, thinking that was great news. "Wait. Let me guess. You solved world hunger. Or…created peace on earth. No, I know. You asked out a boy."

Adi wrinkled her nose. *"Eww…"*

Brock grinned and Adi giggled, the sound music to his ears.

"She wanted to know if I'd be her new mommy," the aide said.

Yikes. Brock sucked in a breath.

"She also asked the lunch lady and vice principal. And the janitor."

Right. Brock rose and took Adi's hand. "Ready to go home, sweetie?"

Finally, a spark of life. "Beep."

CHAPTER SEVEN

WHEN BROCK ARRIVED HOME, the first thing Cassie noticed was how good he looked in his black pants and an azure blue button-down. She'd gone more casual in jeans and a top herself today, her time spent on a series of conference calls with her practice out in California before coming to Brock's to walk the dog. Also, she'd spoken with Brock's staff regarding her consult on the Serene Ogden case. Which reminded her she needed to talk to Brock about that, since they'd scheduled an appointment with the patient at the hospital for the following week to discuss the treatment and reconstruction options.

"Hey." Brock let go of Adi's hand as he closed the door behind them.

"Hey," Cassie said back, her breath catching a little at his crooked smile.

Then his eyes flicked to her lips, and a shot of desire went straight through her, heading south.

Oh, no. No, no, no.

No matter how attractive Brock was, or how he made her knees wobble with just one glance, this thing between them could not go any further. He had a life here and hers was elsewhere. There was no future in it. She repeated that to herself a few times, but her body didn't buy into the hype. Her body still wanted him. Badly.

Brock swung the little girl up and around so he carried her piggyback style. Now there were two faces looking at Cassie, both eerily similar, though Adi's lacked the fine stress lines outside the eyes and the world of knowledge in them.

"My daughter's going to be good today," Brock said. "Aren't you, sweetie?"

Adi nodded. Winnie was at their feet, running in circles, chasing her own tail. With Adi still on board, Brock scooped up the puppy too. "I can't promise the same for the dog."

Winnie panted.

Cassie gave the French bulldog a steely-eyed look, then smiled at Adi. "Hey there, kiddo."

Adi started to answer, but Brock adjusted his hold on the dog and reached back, covering his daughter's mouth.

"Wait," Cassie said, frowning. "I think she was going to use words."

"Trust me, you don't want to hear them."

Adi pulled her father's hand away. "Are you my new mommy?"

Cassie froze, and Adi giggled.

"Okay, sweetie," Brock said, his expression abashed. "You know I love the sound of your laugh, but I will squash you like a grape if you say that to one more person today." He set Adi down and crouched in front of her. "How about you go find something to do that won't get you in trouble?"

When the kid was safely in her room, Brock straightened and looked at Cassie again, his smile conveying gratitude, and a good amount of something else too, something that made her chest squeeze as he led her out the side door for some privacy.

"We should probably have a talk. About Adi."

"Okay." Cassie crossed her arms, sensing something big was coming.

"We've built a nice little life here for ourselves after…" He stopped and took a deep breath. "After everything that happened. My daughter's been through a lot. I don't want her to get hurt again."

"I understand that, and I assure you I have no intention of hurting anyone, Brock." She leaned back against the side of the house. "The only reason I'm here now is because you asked me for a favor. Otherwise, I'd be out looking for a new place to stay."

Brock frowned. "What about your rental?"

"My reservation is up the day after tomorrow and they're already booked after that. With summer and the July Fourth holiday approaching and all the tourists, I was lucky to get it when I did." She sighed. "Madi and Luna both offered to let me stay at their places, but I don't want to impose. I'd get a hotel, but the closest one with any rooms available is nearly back to Boston and I really don't want to commute back and forth for my patient's case if I can avoid it." Cassie straightened. "Which reminds me. I talked to your staff, and they set up a meeting for us with Serene Ogden next week."

"Okay." Brock nodded, looking thoughtful. Then he shoved his fingers through his hair, making it stand up on end. His broad shoulders blocked out the sun and tested the seams of his dress shirt in a way that worked for Cassie, bigtime. "I may have a solution. But first things first. I might have underestimated the time I need you to be here. It could be a little longer than just an hour or two." He dropped his arms to his sides as if they weighed far too much. "The truth is I'm late. I'm overbooked. I could be at the office for a while. I have no idea how long Riley will be at the hospital either. Things are crazy around here. But I trust you and Adi's a good kid, even if she refuses to speak English. She will, however, beep."

He'd spoken in a calm, steady voice, but everything about him screamed exhausted tension. Not to mention how much she knew he disliked asking for help. She was the same way. "How long do you think you'll be?"

Brock didn't move or give away any sign of relief, but his eyes warmed. "Eight at the latest."

Five hours from now. Cassie had no idea what to do with a kid for five hours, but she'd figure it out. "Fine. Maybe I can search online for a new place to stay."

"About that." Brock rested his hand on the doorframe beside her head, leaning into her. Her pulse notched higher, and she swallowed hard. Perhaps her plans to stay distant wouldn't be as easy as she'd thought. He cursed under his breath and shook his head. "I can't believe I'm even going to suggest this."

"Suggest what?" she asked, breathier than intended.

"You could stay in my guesthouse."

That was the proverbial bucket of ice water. Cassie stiffened as best she could in her limited space. "What?"

Brock shook his head and stepped back. "Sounds crazy, right? I know. But it could work. You need a place to stay while you're here. I need someone I trust who can step in when needed to watch Adi who won't make the kid think they're sticking around. You've already promised me no one would get hurt and I'm holding you to that, Cassie." The warning was clear in his voice and his eyes, but then he relaxed a little. "Plus, with you here, we can discuss Serene's case as needed, so…"

"Brock…"

He stood in front of Cassie, all hard lines and tough sinew, wrapped in a double dose of testosterone, and it made it hard to concentrate. Or maybe it was the shock of his offer that blurred the thoughts in her head. Whatever it was, she couldn't seem to form a response.

Brock continued. "The guesthouse isn't anything fancy, only seven hundred and fifty square feet, but it's clean and furnished. What do you think?"

What she thought was this whole idea was insane. Especially after that ill-advised kiss at the retirement center. But the more her brain processed it all, it *did* sound kind of perfect. Besides, with Independence Day in just a couple of weeks, the entire Cape Cod area was inundated. She'd be lucky to find a shack available in town, let alone a whole guesthouse, free of charge. Cassie had meant what she'd said about the other thing too. Nobody would get hurt. She could stay here, interact with Brock and Adi only when necessary, and otherwise just enjoy her visit back home. And he was right about the ease of discussing her new case as well. Win-win. She nodded and leaned her head back to meet his gaze. "All right."

"Are you sure?"

"Yes, I'm sure."

"Good." His expression remained unreadable. "Then there's one last thing we need to address."

Brock had probably shaved that morning, but he already had a five o'clock shadow coming in. And his eyes. Fathomless blue pools, as always, giving nothing away. "That picture on the town's social media." He moved closer again, his hands on Cassie's hips, squeezing slightly before sliding up her sides, past her ribs, to her arms and her shoulders, making her shiver with awareness. By the time he got to her throat and cupped her cheek, her bones seemed to have disappeared. "And what led up to it."

"What are you doing?" she managed to whisper past her constricted vocal cords.

"This." Brock's eyes held hers, purposely building the anticipation, along with the heat inside her. Cassie was in big trouble here, of the going-down-for-the-count kind. Time to wave the white flag. And she would. In just a minute…

He nibbled her lower lip and soothed it with his tongue, then stroked and teased her with his mouth until she let out a helpless murmur of arousal and fisted her hands in his shirt. Brock's eyes were heavy-lidded and sexy when he pulled back. His mouth curved as he looked down.

Following his gaze, Cassie realized she still gripped his shirt. She forced herself to smooth her fingers over the wrinkles she'd made. His gaze went dark with lust and focused on hers, his hands on her back, fingers stroking her through the thin material of her top. When he lowered his head again, he did so slowly, giving her plenty of time to turn away.

She didn't.

Their eyes held until his lips touched hers, then her lashes swept down involuntarily. Cassie couldn't help it; Brock's lips were warm, firm and just right…

With a deep, masculine groan, he threaded his hands through her hair and tilted her head, parting her lips with his, kissing her lightly at first, then not so lightly. Then everything felt insistent and urgent, and time slowed.

By the time Brock broke the kiss, Cassie was unsteady on her feet, and her breathing was more in line with a marathon run. Brock wasn't doing much better, his face flushed and his shirt half-untucked—her doing. He looked danger-ously alluring and hotter than sin.

"I'm not looking for a relationship," he said

quietly, shaking his head. "You've seen my life, Cassie. Hell, you're living it. I'd be crazy to bring someone into this mess. And I can't, because of Adi. I have to be responsible because of her."

"Good. We're on the same page," she said with relief. Except not really. She *should* feel relieved, but didn't, which made no sense. Neither of them wanted this, right? "I meant what I said about not hurting anyone. Least of all your daughter. I don't want a relationship either. My life isn't here in Wyckford anymore. You know that. Why would I start something I can't finish?"

He seemed to consider that, a bit of the tension in his shoulders releasing as his gaze dropped to her mouth and a sexy smile graced his lips. "Understood. Thanks for agreeing to help with Adi."

"Thanks for letting me stay in your guesthouse." Cassie went up on tiptoe so her mouth brushed his with each syllable. This was nuts. This was illogical. This was completely amazing.

Brock groaned and the sound was so innately male, so sensually dominating, that she tingled all over. This was way better than any fantasy Cassie had ever had about this man. She leaned into him, and when Brock groaned, it rumbled from his chest to hers.

In the back of her mind, warning bells clanged, but Cassie shoved them aside. In the last five years, she'd rarely thrown caution to the wind and done something just for her, just because it felt so good in the moment. And while this was only temporary, that didn't mean it couldn't be fun and fantastic. No connections. No hearts or hurt involved. Couldn't get much safer than that, right?

She pulled away, lifting her hands from him, and backed right into the door.

His hand slid up from her lower back until he cupped her head in his palm. "Careful."

They stared at each other. Then like iron to a magnet, she was back in Brock's arms, her hands sliding up his chest, around his neck, until her fingers glided into his hair. He made another sound low in his throat and pulled her into him. Cassie wasn't sure which of them made the next move after that, but they were kissing again, and man, the guy could kiss, *really* kiss—

Brock finally pulled back and nuzzled his face into the soft spot just beneath her ear, whispering, "I need to get back to work."

Once they'd gotten themselves relatively under control, Brock opened the door and Winnie was at their feet, squealing and snuffling, trying to coax someone into picking her up.

"Beep," Adi said from the kitchen.

Cassie's uterus contracted, but that made no sense. She had her future mapped out for at least the next five years. After she'd achieved what she wanted professionally, then she'd think about starting a family.

Brock's phone buzzed and he pulled it from his pocket, mouth grim. "Gotta go."

He took Cassie's hand and led her along with him through the house and out the front. Brock shut the door firmly, then pressed her back against the wall beside it—out of view from inside—and dipped down a little to meet her gaze.

"We have got to stop meeting like this," she said, laughing low, dizzy on desire.

He didn't smile. "Tell me we're on the same page, Cassie."

"The no-relationship page?" she asked. "Yes, we're there."

"If this is going too fast or—"

"No. It's good," she said, doing her best to quell the clambering need inside her. "I'll watch Adi. We'll discuss the case. I'll stay in the guesthouse. No strings. No long-term connections. Promise. This is just for fun."

Neither of them had time for more. Brock didn't want a relationship. He didn't want his daughter hurt. She'd be leaving soon, going back to California. She had a new case to dive into. She didn't want romance and happily ever afters.

Do I?

Instead of contemplating the answer to that question, Cassie changed subjects. "Anything critical I need to know about your daughter?"

"Adi's shy and won't tell you if she's hungry or thirsty. She eats dinner at five-thirty, and there's stuff in the freezer with directions included. Be careful not to deviate—she has food allergies. There's a card on the counter listing all the no-no's. And don't let her feed Winnie any of her toys. That painful lesson cost me six hundred bucks last week."

"Ouch." Cassie winced on behalf of both the bill and the dog. "So feed and water the kid and keep Winnie away from the toys. Got it. We'll be fine, Dr. Turner."

He let out a half laugh. "Are we back to that, Dr. Murphy?"

"Don't you like it when people call you doctor?"

"Only if they're sitting on my exam table."

Cassie looked into Brock's eyes and saw nothing but mild impatience and a lingering heat that stoked hers back into flames. "You need to go."

"Yeah." Except he brushed his mouth over hers again, kissing her with some serious intent before pulling back. "Dammit."

She wobbled unsteadily and had to laugh. "See you when you get home."

"Yes, you will."

CHAPTER EIGHT

BROCK WENT BACK to the office, but as he worked through his patients, all he had to do was look at a door and he'd think about Cassie.

He wanted her, which made no sense, since she was a woman with a life and a busy practice of her own over two thousand miles away. She wasn't looking for love and he wasn't looking to give what was left of his heart away. Maybe that was the appeal. After all, he'd fallen head over heels for Kylie and his life had changed forever because of it. Both good and bad. But love had also given him Adi, which he wouldn't change for the world.

Though he never wanted to relive the pain of loss again.

Which brought him back to his ridiculous attraction to Cassie. She wasn't his type. And okay, so maybe he didn't exactly have a type. His requirements were warm and sweet—except in bed, where he preferred decidedly not warm and sweet. But if he wanted Cassie exactly because he knew ahead of time it wouldn't go anywhere, maybe that made it make more sense? They could have their cake and eat it too, essentially. They'd agreed to be on the same page—the no-relationship, no-emotions, no-messy-connections page. Like grown-ups.

Sometimes he hated being a grown up, but in this instance...

"Room one," Darlene said as they passed each other in the hallway.

Mrs. Carlisle waited on him. She'd accidentally mixed up her blood pressure meds with her husband's erectile dysfunction meds. Unfortunately, she was also hard of hearing. "Mrs. Carlisle, you need to get the pill dispenser we discussed to prevent this from happening."

"What, dear?" she yelled at him, an arthritic hand curled around her ear. "I'm going to grow taller and harder?"

She grinned at her own joke, slapping her knee, completely unconcerned that everyone else in the office could probably also hear her. "My husband's a good man, but he's not built for much downstairs, if you know what I'm saying."

Brock did, but really wished he didn't.

"Aw. Your father would have laughed," Mrs. Carlisle said, giving him a chiding look. "You're not much fun."

Brock's next patient was Kenny Liotta, a long-haul trucker who came in about every six weeks with a new STD. "You ever think about using condoms, Mr. Liotta?"

Kenny grinned. "Your dad used to ask me the same thing. Problem is, I'm not exactly thinking with my brain in these situations."

Brock shook his head and wrote a script. "You need to be more careful, or you could wind up with serious consequences—ones a simple prescription won't cure."

Kenny scoffed. "But what a way to go, right?"

"No," Brock said. "Go with a heart attack of pleasure. Not an STD."

"Yeah, I see your point." Kenny nodded. "You're a good man, Doc. Not going to sell the practice, are you? Like all the others around here have?"

The local hospital's procurement of other county medical facilities was common knowledge. And by absorbing them all under one umbrella, it gave the medical center a huge boost in popularity and reputation. This translated to big bucks for them, of course. Every physician in the area was affiliated with the hospital in some way now. Brock was one of the lone holdouts. "I'm thinking about it. But the level of care here will remain the same."

"You sure?"

"Yes," Brock said firmly. But if he truly believed it, then why hadn't he signed already?

The board didn't understand either. Neither did his friend Mark when he called later that day to see if Brock was ever going to go rock climbing with him again.

"I can't," Brock said. "My schedule here is full."

"You need to get your life under control, dude."

"I know. I'm still thinking."

"Will you still be thinking when you're too old to hang off a cliff without dropping your dentures?"

Brock sighed. "Call Tate. He'll rock climb."

"No, he won't. The guy who jumps out of helicopters to rescue people doesn't like heights."

Brock got home at eight-thirty, half an hour late. Again.

When he'd seen Cassie earlier that day, she'd looked put together in her jeans and top, her hair loose and falling silkily past her shoulders, easy and relaxed. During their moment out back, her hair had gotten mussed—his doing—and her expression hadn't been nearly so calm. Her pupils had been dilated, her mouth swollen and wet from his kisses.

He'd liked that look a lot.

Now, as he walked into his kitchen, Cassie

had pulled her hair up into some sort of knot atop her head, held there by what looked like a swizzle stick, with long strands escaping wildly, making her look a little bit like a mad scientist. Chocolate streaked the front of her shirt, and she was smiling. Before her, on the table, was a tray of completed cupcakes.

"What are those for?" he asked, the day's tension draining from his shoulders. "Sorry I'm late, by the way."

"Turns out Adi needs them for school tomorrow," Cassie said, turning a concerned gaze his way. "Was there an emergency?"

"In the ER. A sixteen-year-old girl pierced her own tongue, and it abscessed. She didn't tell her parents for three days until it swelled, blocking her breathing."

"Oh, God."

"Yeah. She's okay, though. Grounded for life, but okay."

Cassie looked from him to the tray. "Well, it sounds like you could use one of these then. I made two batches, so help yourself."

"Thanks," Brock said, impressed.

The room was a complete disaster, like a bomb had gone off. Dishes piled high in the sink and ingredients everywhere. Lois was still out of town, so he'd be cleaning this mess up later, but he couldn't bring himself to care. "Looks like everyone's still alive too. Where's Adi?"

"Getting ready for bed."

Brock found his daughter in her room, bathed and ready to sleep, Winnie compliant at her feet. Two perfect angels. He tucked Adi in, then crouched beside her bed. "Sleep tight, sweetie," he said, hugging Adi. "Don't let the bedbugs bite."

Adi hugged him back. "'Night, Daddy."

His jaw dropped, the sound of his daughter using actual words again grabbing him by the throat so he couldn't breathe for a second.

After he left his daughter's room, Brock walked back out to the living room where Cassie grabbed her purse, then they walked out of the house together. He turned her to face him. "You got Adi to use words."

"I told her I didn't speak droid. She told me all about that toy she carries everywhere." Cassie smiled. "You've got a great kid, Brock."

"I know. And thanks," he said. "For everything. When are you moving into the guesthouse?"

"Probably tomorrow. We'll see." The moonlight slanted over her features as she looked at him a long moment. "If you don't mind me saying so, your daughter needs more of you."

Brock drew in a slow, deep breath. "I know."

"And Winnie isn't so bad. With some training, I think she'll make a great pet."

"Anything else?"

"I don't know Riley that well, but I think she's going through a lot she doesn't talk about because she doesn't want to burden you." Cassie tilted her face up to his. "You're a great doctor, Brock. Always were. But you're also a control freak. Want me to say more?"

"No. But what am I supposed to do? You've seen my life, Cassie. It's…complicated." His mouth quirked. "My schedule's insane, and I *have* to be a control freak to keep it all managed."

"Which is what makes you a great doctor."

"And a crappy dad," he said. God how he hated *that* admission. "Apparently, a crappy brother too."

Neither of them said anything for a while, until Cassie mentioned carefully, "Like I said, Adi's got a thing tomorrow at school. She's also working on a project. A family tree. But she told me she didn't have any pictures of her mom."

"Adi has pictures of Kylie," Brock said, frowning. "But she doesn't remember her."

"She was just a baby when Kylie died."

"Yes."

He waited for the usual hint of pity in Cassie's hazel eyes.

Brock hated it, both for Adi and himself. They'd done just fine on their own and had moved on as best they could. Well, mostly. Sort of. Okay, maybe not so well, based on what Cassie had just told him. He rubbed at the beginning of a headache right between his eyes.

"You're tired." Cassie patted his arm like he was her patient. "Get some sleep."

He stared down at her, torn between showing her just how awake he still was and wanting her to leave before he did exactly that.

Before she pulled away, he caught her hand.

Cassie stared at their intertwined fingers, sighed, then dropped her forehead to his chest. "Do you have to smell so good?" she asked, voice muffled. "Like, *always*?"

Not what Brock expected her to say. "I—"

"No, don't answer that." She lifted her head and kissed him on the cheek. Her breath was warm, and she still had that sweet cupcake scent about her. Her lips lingered and Brock didn't need an engraved invitation. He turned his head, pressing his mouth to hers.

Oh, yeah. *This*. What he'd needed all day long. His tongue teased the corner of her lip. When she opened for him, hunger took over, setting him on fire. Hauling Cassie up against him, Brock took control of the kiss, deepening it. She rewarded him with a soft moan that said she was right there with him, and he felt a whole lot better.

Finally, Cassie stepped back, laughing at herself. Him too, he suspected, as she got into her car. They were acting like horny teenagers and for whatever wild reason, he was there for it.

Brock watched her drive away, turning only when her taillights disappeared.

CHAPTER NINE

CASSIE WENT BACK to her room at the Airbnb that night and sat on the bed while she checked her e-mails. Staying at Brock's guesthouse really would be more convenient. All she had to do was vow to keep her heart—and her emotions—to herself for the duration of her stay, which hopefully shouldn't be more than a few weeks. She'd gotten the case files on Serene Ogden, which she scanned now.

The patient was a twenty-six-year-old black female with extensive facial injuries due to a motor vehicle accident six months prior. Her upper and lower jaws had been crushed, and she'd had fifteen other fractures in her face and forehead. Brock had done her initial surgeries in the ER to stabilize her jaws and airways, but she would still require more extensive reconstructive surgery to correct the trauma to her face and skull. The neurosurgeon surgeon who'd also been brought in to consult along with Cassie on the case, Sam Perkins, had been correct. This case did seem like a perfect fit for her practice's new METAMORPHOSIS technology to give Serene the best outcome possible. Especially since she was engaged to be married the following spring.

She scrolled through more of the attached documentation and photos to see how much soft tissue had been lost. Thankfully, not much, according to Brock's extensive, detailed notes. He'd done several microvascular free tissue transfers to help preserve what he could in preparation for the future and more major reconstructions. Serene's initial wounds had been debrided of devitalized tissue and foreign bodies forty-eight hours after the accident and Brock had performed open reduction internal fixation with temporary plates on her jaws to allow for reduction of pain and to establish a framework for planning the definitive reconstruction that Cassie was working on now.

Based on what she saw in the files, Serene was an excellent candidate for the METAMORPHOSIS procedures, though the case would be quite involved. Not only would she need to get a radiologist and a CT technologist involved from the staff at Wyckford General, but also her team of biomedical engineers out in California, who had to be ready to make any custom 3-D printed models they might need for implantation. Not to mention all the preparation and measurement and testing that needed to be done ahead of time. In fact, the sooner they started on things, the better. Given the time constraints, moving into Brock's guesthouse tomorrow made the most sense. With his crazy schedule and her need for data and access to his knowledge of the patient's case, she could pick his brain at any time.

And pick other parts of him too, her naughty thoughts put in before she tamped them down.

The next morning, Cassie showered, dressed and checked out of her Airbnb.

She drove to Brock's place. It was early but she had a conference call scheduled for later that morning with her bioengineers in California regarding the 3-D printing for Serene's case, and she wanted to make sure she was set up somewhere with reliable internet by then.

The front door of the house opened before she knocked. Brock was dressed in a T-shirt and basketball shorts, a messenger bag slung over one shoulder and a duffel bag over the other. He was also carrying the cupcakes on a tray and had Adi, with her lunchbox, by the hand.

Both man and little girl looked at Cassie from twin blue gazes, and her heart did a little somersault in her chest before she could stop it. She smiled at Adi. "Have fun today."

Brock eyed Cassie's own luggage. "You're moving into the guesthouse now?"

"If that's okay."

"Absolutely. Just give me a sec to get her all set." He walked with Adi to the end of the block just as a yellow school bus arrived. They both disappeared onto the bus, then after a few minutes, Brock reappeared without the cupcake tray.

"The bus driver's a friend," he said to Cassie when he'd walked back to the house. "She'll make sure Adi gets into school without getting mobbed for her treats." He took the handle of Cassie's wheeled suitcase from her and led her down the path to the guesthouse. "I'm glad you're staying here."

"Me too. I got Serene's case files last night. I went over them, and from your excellent notes I think she'll make a great candidate for our procedure and I'm glad we're working together on this. I figured since she knew you already, it might make the transition of her case a bit smoother. And if you'd like to assist on the surgery, I'd be happy to have you. You always had the best, steadiest hands in our residency cohort, so…" She grinned and then cleared her throat. "I also have a conference call with my team in

California in an hour to discuss starting work on the prosthetics for Serene's case."

"That all sounds great. Thanks." Brock glanced back at her over his shoulder, his gaze making every inch of her tingle and heat, though she did her best to ignore it. "I'll drop your suitcase at the door and give you the key, but whatever you do, don't let me come in with you."

"Why not?" Cassie frowned.

"It would be a bad idea," he said in a voice that scraped over her like plush velvet. "For both of us."

Cassie felt like her whole body went up in flames.

Yeah, he was right. It would be a very bad idea. So any future meeting about the case would need to be outdoors. By the pool, maybe. Neutral territory. Noted.

They stopped on the threshold of the guesthouse, and while Brock fiddled with his keys, Cassie couldn't help noticing how his white T-shirt strained over his biceps and pecs but fell loose over his flat, hard abs. When he unlocked the door, the material stretched tight over his broad back. Then there was his butt in those basketball shorts. Edible. That's how it looked, and she wanted to sink her teeth into—

He turned and caught her staring. She quickly

pretended to be staring at her own feet. "Nice pavers."

"You weren't looking at the pavers. You were looking at my ass."

Cassie sighed. "Okay, fine. I was. But it's impolite of you to point it out."

Brock laughed.

She walked past him into the guesthouse, thinking at least now he couldn't see her burning face.

"Cassie?" he said from behind her.

"Yeah?"

"Your ass is ogle-worthy too."

She bit her lower lip to stop a smile and kept walking. "We're being inappropriate again."

"You started it," he said, remaining purposely in the entryway.

The place was tiny, but cute, with an open concept living room, kitchen and bedroom, all done in soft blues and neutral colors.

"The bed is behind that screen," Brock said, pointing. "The kitchen is minimally supplied. You've got wireless, but the electrical is iffy. Don't run the toaster and the heater at the same time until I work on it this weekend."

Cassie turned to meet his gaze. "Are you really not coming in?"

His eyes darkened, and her body reacted with feminine predictability. "If I come in, you're going to miss your call, and I'm going to miss my workout."

Her heart skipped a beat. "Oh."

His mouth curved very slightly, giving her another of those searing looks that made her knees wobble. "Not in our best interests. Lock the door behind me, Cassie."

When he was gone, she let out a shaky breath and did as he'd said. Then she looked over her new place and felt…right at home. Surprising, that. She'd had a lovely childhood in Wyckford with her father, but she hadn't lived here in years. She loved San Diego with the constant warmth and sun, but realized that while California was fun and fresh, it had never felt like home. Now that she was back in Wyckford though, she felt a sudden urge to unpack and nest. "Temporary," she said out loud to remind herself. "This is only temporary."

She did her Zoom call with her bioengineering team and gave them Serene's initial measurements, though those would change after the exam and consultation. She also set up a second call with her team for afterward to share the updated information. Following her conference call, she checked in with her dad at Sunny Village, then returned to her laptop to sort through her messy inbox. By the time she'd finished tidying it up, it was time to get Adi from the bus.

"Beep," the little girl said in greeting.

"Beep," Cassie said back. "But I was sort of hoping we could use English today too. Because you and I are going to make pizza for dinner."

"I like pizza!"

Cassie smiled and walked Adi home. They worked on the little girl's handwriting and made pizza, and after that, Cassie braided Adi's hair.

"I'm going to be a rebel princess someday," Adi said.

"That's awesome." Cassie worked a comb gently through a particularly stubborn snarl. "What else do you want to be?"

"Besides a rebel princess?" Adi frowned.

Cassie rested her chin on the little girl's shoulder as Adi sat cross-legged on her lap. "Yes. Girls can be lots of things at once. You can make art and do science and dance and sing if you want." She stroked a lock of dark hair back from Adi's face. "Whatever you decide to do and be, you'll be amazing."

Adi beamed from the compliment, then went back to playing with her droid. "But if I'm princess, then I'll be so powerful I can bring my mommy back to life."

That got Cassie right in the feels. She didn't talk much after that for fear of crying. She'd lost her own mother young, so she knew how it felt to miss what you never knew. She hugged Adi tighter when she finished with her braids, then sent the little girl to her room to play on her own.

Brock got home at eight, looking hot as usual in wrinkled dark blue scrubs and athletic shoes, his hair rumpled, his eyes tired and unguarded. Adi and Winnie jumped him on the spot, and the three of them wrestled on the floor like a pack of wolves until suddenly Adi sat straight up, looking green.

"Uh-oh," she said, and threw up all over her father.

Brock handled the situation with calm efficiency, scooping his distraught daughter up, cleaning up the mess and himself, then corralling the crazy puppy who ran worried circles around a sniffling Adi. Finally, Brock sat his freshly changed daughter on the kitchen counter and handed her a glass of water. "What did you have for dinner?"

"Pizza," Cassie said. "No pepperoni. It was on the list. Just turkey sausage."

"Did you check the label on the back though? Sometimes they slip things into the sausage, and Adi's allergic to pork."

"Oh, damn." Cassie looked at the little girl, who was clutching her droid and staring at her bare feet. "I didn't. I'm sorry. Do we need to take her to the ER?"

"I think the vomiting took care of it," Brock

said, smiling down at his daughter. "I checked her temperature and its normal, and there's no sign of swelling either. But I'll keep an eye on her for the next hour or so to be sure. Any sign of Riley?"

"She called and said she had to work late again."

Brock sat at the kitchen island and colored with Adi while Cassie busied herself picking up the disaster the house had somehow become over the past few hours. Brock had mentioned his housekeeper was due back from Italy the following week and Cassie didn't want the woman to have a coronary when she saw the place. In the living room, in the middle of the chaos, Winnie lay on the couch on her back, her feet straight up in the air like she was dead, snoring away.

"You don't have to clean up," Brock said, stopping her tidying by taking Cassie's hand in his as she passed by him in the kitchen and pulling her around to face him. Their gazes locked and time stuttered to a stop for a second, filled with yearning, aching…

Or maybe that was just Cassie.

Stop it.

Brock broke the spell when he noticed Winnie on the sofa, looking like roadkill. "How the hell did she learn how to get up on the couch?"

Cassie almost said because Adi had spent the

better part of an hour teaching the puppy how to jump that high, but instead walked over to nudge a sleepy Winnie down, earning a reproachful look and a soft snort.

Clearly, she'd done enough here for the night. She grabbed her purse and headed for the door.

"Cassie—"

"Don't forget our consult with Serene on Friday," she said, ready to change the subject, still discombobulated by the fact she'd somehow let her feelings slip through. She'd have to be much more careful about that going forward. Must be fatigue. Yep. That was it. She turned back to Brock as she opened the door. "It's late. I need to get some rest. Goodnight. See you tomorrow."

CHAPTER TEN

THURSDAY NIGHT WHEN Brock got home, Adi was just getting out of the tub. Cassie hurried to get her things together, which Brock knew was to give him some alone time with his daughter.

Or else she wasn't all that interested to be in his company.

If it was the latter, that was probably for the best.

"Adi-bean," he said, "get into your pj's and pick out a book. I'll be right back. Give me five minutes." Then he jogged through the house and caught up with Cassie at the back door. "Hey."

"Hey." She gave him a sweet smile, even if it didn't quite meet her eyes. "Ready for our consult tomorrow?"

"I am." Unable to resist touching her, Brock caught her hand in his. "But I also wanted to make sure you were okay, after you left so fast the other night."

She went still as he turned her to face him,

her expression unreadable. "I was tired. But I'm better now."

"Okay, good."

This time when she smiled at him, it looked genuine.

"How did today go?" he asked.

"Good. We had our weekly practice meeting with my colleagues in California. Went over my patient roster for when I return."

Brock's chest tightened then with something—regret? Longing?—before he shook it off. "That's great."

"Yeah." Her enthusiasm sounded a little forced, or maybe that was just his wishful thinking. It was, after all, her future, and he knew how much Cassie loved her work. He wanted Cassie to be happy. She deserved it. But he also wanted to stop thinking about it, and so Brock distracted himself with the view.

Today, Cassie wore jeans and a light-yellow sweater. The color brought out the green in her hazel eyes. Her hair was loose again, and soft waves fell over her shoulders and down her back. She looked a little rumpled and very warm and soft, not so perfect and poised, more…human. Just a regular woman, a woman who did her best for her patients and her father and those she cared for. Brock admired her greatly for her generous spirit. He also wanted to hug her.

Brock reached up to push a lock of hair off Cassie's forehead, then caught himself, saying quietly, "Thanks for including me on Serene's case. She's a special patient. I think you'll see that as well when you meet her tomorrow."

She stared at his chest. "No need to thank me. You did amazing work after her accident, Brock. And your notes were—"

"Arf arf arf!" came Winnie's bark through the open back door.

"Beep beep beep!" came Adi's voice from the kitchen.

Brock dropped his forehead to Cassie's shoulder and sighed.

"She spoke English all day," Cassie said. "Until you came home."

He lifted his head and looked at her again. "So it's me then."

Cassie hesitated, as if knowing she had to tell him bad news but wanted to cushion the blow. "You know she wants to be a princess, right?"

"Everyone in Wyckford knows she wants to be Princess Leia."

"Yes, but did you know why? Adi told me she wants to be her because she thinks then she'll be powerful enough to bring her mother back to life." Cassie sighed. "I know what that's like, Brock. Losing your mom so young. She just needs time and support. You can give her that. Like my dad gave me."

Brock blinked, then closed his eyes, his heart clogging his throat, and all the pain of the last five years choked his breath away. Then the barking increased in intensity, and he pulled free. He was needed again, because someone, somewhere always needed him. Except who was there when Brock needed someone himself? "I have to go."

"I know," Cassie said, her smile resigned. "See you tomorrow at the consult."

The next morning, Cassie woke up early. It was chilly, so she cranked on the heat and then went to the kitchen to search for breakfast. While trying to decide between yogurt or a bagel, she thumbed through her messages on her phone, stopping at one from her father:

Hi, honey. We could use you as a model again this afternoon if you're free. Talk to you soon. Love, Dad

Half-awake and still staring at the text, Cassie popped a bagel into the toaster. Something sizzled, then the lights went out.

Oh, crap.

Brock's warning came back to her, a little too late.

Don't use the heater and the toaster at the same time.

There wasn't much light to see by, just the predawn gloom filtering in through the windows. No flames though, at least ones she could see. Concerned about fire in the walls, Cassie threw on a robe and ran for the big house. The back door was locked, but she saw Adi sitting at the kitchen table with Winnie in her lap through the window. They were sharing cereal out of the same huge plastic container. Not a surprise since Winnie loved anything edible. Especially if Adi was eating it.

Cassie waved. Winnie jumped off Adi's lap and barreled through the kitchen. Losing traction, the dog slid on the tile floor and crashed face-first into the back door. Bouncing back on her butt, Winnie sat there a moment, dazed, before shaking her head and barking again.

Cassie sighed and caught Adi's eye, gesturing to the locked door.

The little girl waved back.

"Come open the door, please," Cassie called.

Adi eventually did.

Winnie was still barking.

"Where's your dad?" she asked the little girl.

Adi pointed vaguely toward the hall and

Cassie headed that way. The first door—Adi's—was open, revealing a bedroom that looked like a disaster zone of epic proportions.

The next door, Riley's, was shut.

Brock's room was at the end of the corridor, his door partially open, allowing Cassie to peek in. And, oh, my... He was sprawled out flat on his back in the middle of the bed, shirtless, the covers riding low enough on his hips to reveal a mouthwatering chest, abs to die for and a happy trail that vanished beneath the sheet and made Cassie want to do the same.

He was probably naked, and the thought gave her a hot flash. "Brock?"

He didn't move, so Cassie padded barefoot over to the bed and touched his shoulder. Before she could say his name again though, Brock grabbed her wrist and tugged, sending her sprawling over him, and then he rolled her beneath him.

And yep, he was naked.

"Mmm..." Brock rumbled. "Like the robe. It's soft."

She let out a breathless laugh, her hands wandering over his shoulders and back because, hello, she was only human. He was warm and solid and felt so good nuzzling her neck. Not at all sure he wasn't still in dreamland, Cassie nudged him. "You awake?"

"Yeah." He sighed. "And Adi's probably up."

Brock was "up" too, and the thought gave her a shiver of arousal. "Adi's eating cereal out of the same container as your dog."

"Perfect." Brock rolled off her then stood—still very naked—and grabbed a pair of jeans off a chair to pull them on, adjusting himself and giving her another hot flash.

Cassie looked away quick and lost her train of thought, her attention still riveted to the part of him that was the *most* awake.

Stop it. Cassie. You came here for a reason.

"I've got a problem."

"What now?" He finished buttoning his fly and stood there, hair tousled, no shirt, no socks, nothing but those low-riding jeans, and wow, it was hard to think. "I turned on the heater and—"

Brock groaned. "Not the toaster."

"And the toaster." She winced. "I'm worried about a fire."

"Dammit." He headed out the door with Cassie on his heels. Adi tagged along as well, wanting to see the "big flames!"

Luckily there was no fire. Turns out she'd only tripped an electrical breaker, but she'd learned her lesson. And that lesson was, don't go to Brock's bedroom or she'd see things she wanted but shouldn't have.

"I wanted to put out the big flames with the Force," Adi said, disappointed. "That'd make me the bestest ever." She paused. "After you, Daddy. 'Cause you're the first bestest."

Cassie's heart cracked in two, and she looked at Brock. He crouched before his daughter, hands on Adi's skinny little hips while she stared down at her light-up sneakers.

Brock put a finger beneath his daughter's chin and gently tilted up her face. "You're already the best daughter there is, sweetie. The very best."

"But I wish I could bring Mommy back. I want a mommy."

For a moment, Brock didn't say anything. Then, when he spoke, his voice was a little hoarse and filled with conviction. "I know you miss her, sweetie. I miss her too. Someday, we'll find the right person for our family. Until then, it's you and me, kid. Okay?"

"Okay." Adi nodded. "And you're still the bestest, Daddy."

When Brock opened his arms, his daughter walked right into them and curled into his chest.

Cassie stopped herself from crawling into Brock's arms too.

But she wanted to. And that was not good.

That afternoon, Cassie walked into Wyckford General Hospital and had a serious case of déjà vu. Some things were the same, like the noise and the hustle and the full waiting room for the ER, but other things were different, like many of the faces around her. She and Brock took the elevator up to the sixth floor where their conference room was located and entered a contemporary-style room full of beige and cream chairs and a long white oak table. Cassie set her laptop at one end while Brock got the Bluetooth AV equipment set up so she could sync with it.

"Serene's bringing her fiancé with her today," Brock said after giving Cassie a thumbs-up for the digital projector. "His name is Rodney."

"Perfect. Having a good support system will really help with her recovery."

"Exactly."

Before they could say anything more, a knock announced their patient's arrival.

Cassie set her bag aside and stood as Serene Ogden and her fiancé entered the office. Brock exchanged hugs and pleasantries with them, then led them over to the table for introductions.

"I'm so glad to be working with you again, Serene and Rodney," Brock said. "And this is my colleague from California, Dr. Cassandra Murphy."

"Hello." Cassie shook their hands, then took a seat beside Brock, opposite Serene and Rodney. "Dr. Turner has said he told you a little about why I'm here, but I'd like to explain more to you both about our METAMORPHOSIS technology and how I think it can help you have the best outcome here, Ms. Ogden."

"Serene, please."

"Okay, Serene." Cassie smiled. "First off, why don't you both tell me a little bit about yourselves?"

"Well," Serene said. "I'm twenty-six and a schoolteacher. Or I was, until this happened." She gestured toward her face. "And I'm engaged to marry the best man in the whole world." Serene reached over and squeezed Rodney's hand.

Rodney kissed her on the cheek. "And I'm Rodney Bennett. I'm a manager at the new fulfillment warehouse over near Brookline. Been there about four years now. Saving up for a down payment on a house for us once we get hitched."

"Nice," Cassie said. "My father used to live near Brookline, before he went into a retirement community."

"Really?" Rodney grinned. "Good area."

"Yeah." Cassie reached down into the bag at her feet and pulled out a folder with information for Serene. "Right. Well, let's get started, shall we? We're going to cover a lot of things today in a short period of time. If you need me to slow down or if you have questions, please let me know. Dr. Turner and I are here to help you both. We want to make this whole experience as painless as possible."

"I'm all for painless," Serene said, smiling with the left side of her face. The right side was still drooping and paralyzed, but Cassie and her procedure would hopefully take care of that.

"Good."

Brock handed Cassie the remote and she turned to click on the presentation he'd loaded for her earlier. Onscreen, the METAMORPHOSIS logo shimmered, then a photo of Serene taken before she'd left the hospital months earlier appeared. Next to it was a CGI rendition of what the technology predicted Serene would look like after the procedures were all completed. Night and day. Cassie explained what surgeries would be involved and the risks and benefits of using the virtual planning and 3-D printing for custom prosthetics for Serene.

About an hour later, Cassie wrapped up her presentation and clicked the monitor back to the side-by-side photos of Serene. "Any questions for us?"

"Will you be doing all this yourself, Dr. Murphy?" Serene asked.

"Yes. My team in California is already working on prototypes for us to start with. They'll make better ones after I take specific measurements today. And they'll continue to have input on the case as we move forward. Also, I've asked Dr. Turner to assist on the surgery since he's familiar with your case," Cassie said, glancing over at Brock. "But yes, I'll be doing the major facial reconstructive parts of the procedure myself. And I'll bring in a local maxillofacial surgeon to handle work around your jawline and your new dental implants. And a neurosurgeon will also be there to make sure the facial nerves are reconstructed properly as well. You'll sit down for consults with them both also prior to the surgery to answer any questions you might have for their parts. Again, I'll coordinate all that."

"And Serene and Rodney, my door is always open—for whatever you need," Brock added. "Even if it's just a pep talk. I know how important support can be in difficult situations. And the billing department here at the hospital is already working on your case. Since this is part of a case study, Dr. Murphy's practice is going to cover most of the cost of the procedure, but if there's anything left over, we'll find ways to cover that for you. Our main priority here is to get you your life back. And get you ready for your wedding next spring."

"Thanks, Dr. Turner," Serene and Rodney said in unison, both smiling. Then they turned to Cassie and hugged her. "And thanks, Dr. Murphy. I've been waiting for this day for so long."

"Any other questions right now?" Cassie asked, smiling. "Take the information I gave you home and read through all the information. If you do think of anything I haven't answered for you, please call me and we'll discuss further." Serene and Rodney both nodded. "Okay. Well, if you don't have any more questions, I'll send you next door to the exam room, Serene, so we can get started."

After the exam was finished and the patient and her fiancé had left, Brock and Cassie sat at the conference table alone. Brock was struck by how easy and natural this felt, working with Cassie again, even after all these years. It was like they'd fallen back into the same team dynamic they'd always had together. Complementing each other's styles like two interlocking puzzle pieces. He'd missed that more than he realized. "Thanks again for involving me in all this."

"Of course. I know how busy your schedule is already, so I appreciate you taking the time to do this." Cassie folded her hands on the table in front of her, frowning. "I also hope it won't bring up too many painful memories from your past. I didn't realize until today how dealing with another car accident patient might affect you."

Brock swallowed hard. He hadn't either. To be honest, he'd expected to maybe have some flashbacks or something to Kylie and his parents, but so far there'd been nothing. Maybe time had started to heal his wounds. Or maybe the woman across from him had something to do with it too.

Careful there.

He cleared his throat and sat forward to rest his forearms on the table, changing subjects. "Maybe we should talk through the next steps in the process to ensure we're both on the same page?"

Cassie nodded and picked up a picture of Serene and Rodney from the file, taken just days before the accident. "She was a beautiful woman, and her smile was amazing."

Brock was determined to see Serene smile like that again.

"It won't be easy to restore her to exactly the same as she was before her injuries though," Cassie said, putting the photo back and opening the tablet computer on the table. "And, according to her file, she's already had several procedures to handle the osseous reconstruction, which is healing nicely, but now we'll get into the delicate facial soft tissue reconstruction. The most challenging part."

"And your specialty." Brock looked at the

large flat-screen monitor on the wall, where Cassie's graphics were displayed. She clicked a few keys on the keyboard to rotate the 3-D model of Serene's skull on the screen as they discussed the intricate details of the surgery to come.

"It's going to be complicated," Cassie said, her hazel eyes lit with sudden fire. "But I already promised the patient I'd do it, and I never go back on a promise."

"No," Brock said, smiling. "You don't."

It was true. For as long as he'd known Cassie, she'd always been loyal and trustworthy to a fault. Another reason he was glad to have her helping him with the dog and Adi. Also, it was nice spending time with another adult, besides his sister, again. He'd missed real conversations and quiet support. It had been too long since Brock had had either.

They continued talking through the procedure and their recommendations on how to fix the patient's injuries for the best results. By the time they finished, several hours had passed and the sun was beginning to set outside the office windows. Brock turned off the presentation and began to put away his notes while Cassie yawned and stretched in her chair. He studiously avoided noticing how her white lab coat pulled taut across her slim, yet curvy form, and how shapely her long legs were when she rotated her ankles before standing.

Even if she had ended up in his bed that morning.

Good God.

Forcing those thoughts of how she'd felt beneath him from his mind, Brock closed his folder of notes, picked up his tablet and shoved his desire down deep. Now was not the time.

"I have another call scheduled with my team in California to get them these updated measurements from Serene's exam today. They'll tweak the 3-D CT scanning and processing software to match the new numbers, then do the same with the other software for manipulation and surgical simulation, stereolithographic modeling, customized plating systems, splints and cutting guides, prefabricated implants, and real-time intraoperative surgical navigation for us to use as practice before the big day."

"I have to say, I'm excited to observe your new process," Brock said, waiting near the door for her. "I think having patient-specific practice materials will really help us get the best outcome for Serene. Not to mention cut down on our operative planning and execution time."

"It is quite remarkable," Cassie agreed.

"Agreed." Brock crossed his arms while she finished packing up her things. Thankfully, they had nowhere to go but home after this. A rare treat indeed. They left the conference room together and boarded an elevator, Brock holding the door for Cassie, then pressing the button for the lower-level garage where the physician parking was located.

As the elevator descended, the flashbacks started. His stomach dropped as images of Kylie flashed in his head. Maybe Cassie was right. Maybe his old wounds weren't healed. Maybe they were just lurking in the shadows, waiting to strike. He still remembered sitting in the ER as the doctors told him Kylie's heart had stopped on the exam table. She'd been under the water too long. She'd also had extensive internal injuries. There was nothing they could do. The same old icy fingers of dread squeezed his chest tight now, along with survivors' guilt and remorse. Things he'd thought he'd put to rest a long time ago. Or maybe he'd just buried it all under his impossible schedule and an obsession to stay busy all the time so he didn't have to feel.

"Everything okay?" Cassie asked, jarring Brock back to the present. He hadn't realized how quiet he'd gotten until she said something.

"Uh, yeah. Fine," he said, a bit too quickly. "Just looking forward to a relaxing night for a change."

"I bet." Cassie's warm smile thawed the cold

inside him and had Brock wondering if having her stay in the guesthouse was such a wise decision after all.

CHAPTER ELEVEN

THE NEXT MORNING, a knock at her door had Cassie up early. She looked out the glass into the dawn's purple glow and her heart stumbled. Brock stood there, dressed for his office in dark pants, a dark slate button-down and a dark edgy expression.

She opened the door and stepped back to let him inside, but he shook his head.

Right. He wasn't coming in. Because it was a *bad idea.* Disappointed, Cassie started to close the door, but found it blocked. By Brock, who'd apparently changed his mind. Her hands went to his chest, and the warm strength of him radiated through his shirt.

She couldn't help touching him. He had a great chest. Great abs too. Then there were those side muscles, the obliques, the ones that made even smart women stupid.

"Cassie." His voice sounded husky and a little

tight as he grabbed her hands, making her realize they'd been headed south.

At the connection of his body to hers, she heard herself whimper, the sound shocking her in its need and hunger. "Sorry," she whispered. "I don't think I'm fully awake yet."

His eyes held hers as his free hand glided down her leg, then beneath the hem of her nightshirt. "Maybe this will help."

Before she could respond, he lowered his head and covered her mouth with his in a gentle kiss. Then not so gentle, and when she kissed him back, his growl reverberated deep inside her—a soulful, hungry sound that made her go weak.

"What the hell are we doing, Cassie?" he asked, his voice thrillingly rough when he pulled back.

"Having fun." She tugged him back to her.

Apparently, her answer worked because he kissed her again, his mouth open on hers, igniting flames along her every nerve ending. Her arms wound around his neck and her hands glided into his soft, silky hair.

His hands were just as possessive, going straight to her bottom, squeezing, then lifting her up.

The only barriers between them were his pants and her panties since her nightshirt was now hiked up around her waist. An inkling of common sense niggled its way to the surface of Cassie's brain, and she tore her lips from Brock's to ask, "Adi? Where's Adi?"

"Already on the bus." His mouth was busy at her ear, his movements masculine and carnal, arousing her almost beyond bearing.

"Riley—" she gasped.

"Just left for work." He locked the door.

The click of it sliding home hung in the air alongside their heavy breathing as they stared at each other through the shadows.

"So we're doing this? We're—" Cassie broke off on a startled gasp when Brock tugged her nightshirt over her head. "Okay," she breathed on a shaky laugh. "We're doing this."

With a rough groan, he dipped his head and kissed her collarbone. Then lower. When he licked her nipple as if she were a decadent dessert, Cassie sighed in sheer pleasure.

Brock pulled back to blow lightly on her wet skin, eliciting a bone-deep shiver.

"What about your office?" she murmured, unbuttoning his shirt. In her impatience, she tore off two buttons. "You'll be late."

He didn't answer, his mouth on her once more, gliding from one nipple to the other, then gently nibbling.

Quivering from head to toe, Cassie arched into him, giving him more access. *Brock?*

"You're right," he said, his hand moving between her thighs, rocking against her. "I'm going to be late."

She let out an unintelligible sound, and he lifted his head. "Tell me this is what you want, Cassie. Or I'll stop. I promise. Even though I'm right where I want to be." He kissed his way to the outer shell of her ear, his breath hot, chasing a shiver down her spine.

"I want this too," she said, pressing against him. "I want you."

Then she pulled off his shirt and ran her fingers over his abs, which quivered at her touch. He had one hand on her ass, the other on her breast. She was halfway to orgasm and laughing.

So was he.

Their eyes met then, and the humor faded, replaced by driving need. Turning, Brock gently lowered her onto the couch before he followed her down, covering her body with his own as he kissed her, his fingers tracing the edge of her panties, then beneath.

"Your eyes, Cassie," he said against her mouth. "They show everything."

She gasped when he slid a finger into her, then two, his thumb stroking right over the center of her gravity. "Oh, God."

"Good?"

She bit his shoulder instead of crying out with

exactly how wonderful it was. The pressure built shockingly fast as he stroked her. "Brock—"

He kissed her deep, his tongue moving in the same unhurried motion as his fingers. Cassie writhed beneath him, lost. When she climaxed, she called his name as she rode the wave.

He stayed with her to the end, patient enough to let her come down at her own speed. When she finally blinked up at him, Cassie didn't know whether to be embarrassed or thank him. "How long has it been since you did this?"

"A year and two months."

"You don't seem out of practice."

"Like riding a bike." He slid down her body and hooked his fingers in the sides of her panties that sat low on her hips and slowly pulled them down her legs. Then Brock put a big palm on each leg and spread them for his viewing pleasure. Leaning in, he kissed first one inner thigh, then the other. Then in between.

Cassie couldn't even remember her own name at that point. She rocked up into his mouth, biting her lip to keep quiet. But she was still making noises, horrifyingly needy noises, and little hurry-up whispers and pants as she peaked again. "Oh, God."

He kissed his way up her body. "'Oh, God' good?"

"Amazing."

"Amazing works…" Brock held himself above her on one forearm.

She met his gaze and saw the seriousness there. Cassie's heart sank. "What?"

"I don't have any condoms."

She stared at him. "*What?*"

His laugh was low and a little wry. "You heard the part about a year and two months, right?"

She let out a disappointed breath, body still humming, mind whirling.

"It's okay." His smile was tight as he shifted, making her extremely aware he was still wound up hard. Sitting up, she pushed him back and straddled him.

"Cassie—"

"Shh." She kissed her way down his incredible chest, paying special homage to the many muscles she came across. When she scraped her teeth over one of his flat nipples, he sucked in a breath. His head fell back on the couch cushions as he let out a heartfelt groan, his hands going straight to her ass. "Since you're already late…"

For her, after years of fantasizing, his entire body was an erotic playground. She spent a moment on his abs, licking him like a lollipop, then slid to her knees on the hardwood floor between his spread legs. His erection strained against the front of his pants. She unbuttoned, unzipped and slid her hands inside before wrapping them around his impressive length. This elicited another rough moan from Brock. Leaning over him, she took him into her mouth, prompting him to slide his hands in her hair and—

His phone went off.

He cursed hoarsely.

She readjusted her grip on him and tried again. His fingers tightened in her hair, not to dominate but to direct her. He groaned, and... his phone buzzed again.

"Dammit!" He let her go to fish through his pocket, pulling out his device and glaring at it, then sagged back and stared up at the ceiling.

She rose and looked at him. "Problem?"

"I have to go." But he didn't move.

"Now?"

"Yeah." He let out a slow breath, straightened and pulled her into his lap. He held her close for a minute, kissed her shoulder, then her neck. When he was done, he kissed her mouth before setting Cassie on the couch next to him. Brock got to his feet and fixed his pants situation, which was easier said than done given his current state. Shaking his head, he grabbed his shirt from the floor. He put it on inside out, swore, yanked it off, then righted it and tried again.

"You're going to work like that?" she asked,

gathering her nightshirt from the back of the sofa and pulling it on.

He cringed down at his fly. "That bad?"

"Scouts could camp in there."

They both laughed. Cassie tried to remember all the reasons why this thing between them would never work, but at that moment she couldn't. Since all she wanted to do was tug down his pants and finish what she started. Then spend the next few hours cuddled into his side, talking and dozing and maybe repeating all this again.

"Cassie," Brock said on a groan, closing his eyes. "Don't look at me like that. I'm standing here trying to mentally recite chemical elements to calm down, and you're looking at me like you want to eat me for breakfast."

She slapped a hand over her eyes. "Sorry."

His hands gripped her arms and hauled her up against him to kiss her. Then he whispered, "Are we still okay with this arrangement?"

Cassie did her best to sound certain, even though she felt too much to be sure. "Yes."

"Good." Brock let her go. His cell phone was vibrating again, and he was already on it before the door shut behind him.

CHAPTER TWELVE

FOR THE NEXT twelve hours, Brock was up to his eyeballs in patients with the flu and strep throat. Throat cultures and breathing treatments became his favorite words. By 6:00 p.m., he was practically swaying on his feet in exhaustion.

"We done?" he asked Darlene, knowing he still had to face the mountain of paperwork on his desk. "Anyone left to see?"

"No." She knocked on wood. "Don't jinx it. Run while you can."

"What about Mrs. Preston? Didn't I see her on the schedule earlier?"

"She was here, but she got tired of waiting. Said she'd be back another day."

"What brought her in?" he asked.

"Headache. Probably because she'd lost her glasses. She said she'd get another pair from Walmart later instead of bothering you."

Brock spent twenty minutes at his desk facing the torturous pile of documentation he had to do before he was paged into the ER. One of the other doctors couldn't show up for the first half of their night shift, and they needed Brock to fill in. He called Riley, who informed him she was also pulling an extra shift in radiology and couldn't babysit Adi. So he called Cassie. "I hate to ask, but—"

"Don't worry. I've got Adi right here. We're just getting back."

"Back?"

"We went to the playground."

"Really?" An odd emotion blossomed in Brock's chest, sweet and warm and scary enough that he didn't want to identify it just then. Surrounded by hell, his life completely not his own, he found himself smiling for the first time in days as he remembered their tryst earlier that morning. He said softly, "I owe you."

"Sounds promising, Dr. Turner. Talk to you later."

Brock was still smiling when he headed into the ER. The shift was a little crazy, but that was the nature of the beast in any hospital. What kept him sane, and what had drawn him to medicine in the first place, was that no matter how crazy things got in the moment, there was a purpose to all of it, a reason for every orchestrated movement in the treatment room. As a man who liked control, he loved that aspect of science. The routine. The predictability. Even though the patients and cases changed regularly, how he handled them was the same.

If only he could exert that same kind of control over the rest of his life. Over this crazy thing with Cassie. Because despite the rules they'd set for their relationship, or lack thereof, he found things shifting, changing, bending under the sizzling weight and heat of the chemistry between them. Found himself getting drawn deeper into Cassie—the way she smiled, the sound of her laugh, the way she helped others and how everything she did seemed to come from the bottom of her heart. He loved her commitment, her dedication and the purpose behind everything she did.

And if he wasn't careful, it would be easy for him to love her too. And that was unacceptable. Because she was leaving. Because he had to think of Adi and how awful it would be for his daughter to lose another person she'd come to depend on. Because Brock feared his own battered heart wouldn't survive another crushing time through the wringer.

With Cassie it could be different...

But could it though? Brock couldn't see how, with Cassie in town only until the surgery was over. She had a bright, beautiful life back in San Diego, one she'd worked hard to build. Why the hell would she choose this place over that? Brock wasn't sure *he'd* choose it if he'd had a choice.

He didn't have a choice though. This was the hand he'd been dealt, and he would keep charging forward and doing the best he could for his daughter and his sister and for all those who depended on him because that's what he was here for. That was his purpose. That was his destiny.

This thing with Cassie was just a pleasant diversion. A fun break. She'd said so herself.

That was their agreement. And Brock would stick to it, no matter what.

He sighed and checked the roster on the wall for his next waiting patient.

It was 1:00 a.m. before he left the ER. He had a few hours to get home and sleep before the madness started again.

He was halfway to his car when he got the call.

Mrs. Preston had just come in. DOA. Dead on arrival.

No. Dammit!

He'd had a bad feeling about her that afternoon but had pushed it aside because he'd been so behind at the office. He should've called Mrs. Preston, should've checked in on his patient. Should've...

Brock ran back into the hospital, but of course,

there was no rush. Not for the dead. He grabbed the chart. There'd be no official cause of death until the autopsy, but all signs pointed to an aneurysm.

Christ.

Brock stared down at the older woman's body in disbelief. The possibility of a serious medical condition had never been on his radar, even though she'd complained of a headache earlier. He'd put it down to her age, to her constant need for attention and reassurance, to her needing new glasses, like she'd said. Brock had known her patient history by heart and there'd been no sign of something like this. Over the years, he'd probably spent a total of *months* talking to her. He knew she liked her margaritas frozen, her music soft and jazzy and that she had a secret stash of sticky notes. She didn't have much family or any pets, she'd always said she was allergic to both, and she'd never missed a single episode of *The Bachelor*. She'd planned on applying for the senior version of the show someday.

Soon as she could get over her fear of flying to get to LA.

And now she was dead.

Logically, Brock knew it wasn't his fault, but he still felt guilty as hell. Sick too. *Sick* that he'd blown off her case because of his stupid, insane schedule. Sick that he hadn't even taken the time to call and check up on her. Sick that he hadn't insisted she be worked in sooner so she'd have waited for him. Because if he had examined her, maybe he would've caught the aneurysm in time, maybe he'd have somehow known that today wasn't just another ploy for attention and that she'd had a real medical emergency this time. He hadn't even gotten to say good-bye. Again.

Old grief mixed with his new self-recriminations, making him feel lead-heavy and full of regret. Brock touched her hand, then tucked it under the blanket alongside her body. "I'm so sorry, Mrs. Preston. So very sorry."

Only silence greeted him. Devastated him. Still in his scrubs, he drove home in a fog and found Cassie asleep on his living room couch. She sat up, sleepy, rumpled, and flashed him an apologetic smile. "Sorry. Didn't mean to fall asleep."

He helped her to her feet, then shoved his hands into his pockets, not trusting himself to touch her right now. She gave him a curious stare as he walked her back to the guesthouse.

"Brock?" Standing at her door, bathed in the moonlight, she touched his face. "What's wrong?"

Her hazel eyes shimmered, and as always, he

knew if he looked into them for too long, he'd drown.

But he was already drowning. Drowning in everything he'd done wrong, and how this felt so very, very right. She shifted closer, and her body brushed his. Soft. Warm. He could bury himself in her right now and find some desperately needed oblivion.

But taking his grief out on her would be the wrong thing to do. "I'm fine."

He waited until Cassie disappeared into the guesthouse before he returned to the main house, a hurricane of conflicting emotions still swirling inside himself.

Brock didn't go to bed, even though he was more exhausted than he could remember being in a while. Nope. Tonight, he needed a more powerful way to help him forget it all. He went to the cabinet above the fridge for the bottle of bourbon and shot glass he kept hidden there, then to the couch where Cassie had fallen asleep waiting for him. The blanket was still warm from her body heat and smelled like her.

He inhaled deeply and poured himself a shot.

He'd lost track of how much he'd drunk by the time someone knocked softly on the glass slider. When he didn't move, Cassie let herself in.

Brock kept his eyes lowered as she approached, watching her through his lashes. She wore a camisole and cropped leggings. No shoes. Her hair was down. No makeup. He wanted to tear off her clothes, toss her on the couch and bury himself so deep inside her that he couldn't think anymore.

Couldn't feel anymore.

Because the emotions inside him weren't allowed. Not according to their agreement. Things like yearning and needing and lov—

Brock cut off that last one. Even thinking it might make it spill over for her to see and that would be breaking his promise. He couldn't break his promise. Not to her.

So, he sat there and watched her cross the room instead.

But some of his thoughts must've been obvious because Cassie stopped just out of his reach and gave him a long, assessing look. "Saw that the lights were still on," she said. "You can't sleep."

It wasn't a question, so he didn't bother answering. Just shrugged and tossed back another shot. "I lost a patient tonight."

"Oh, Brock. I'm so sorry." She sank down on the sofa cushion next to his. "Madi texted me earlier and told me about Mrs. Preston. Such a sweet older lady."

He went still, giving her some side-eye.

She paused. "You're a good man, Brock. A good doctor. Don't blame yourself for her death."

Too late.

"It wasn't your fault."

Maybe not. But plenty of other stuff *was*. Like Adi thinking she had to be a princess to bring back her dead mother. Like his dad's practice getting too big and losing the personal attention each patient deserved...

Like Kylie. Out driving that night because he'd forgotten a file at home, which she'd been bringing it to him at the hospital. And now she was dead, and it was all his fault.

And like Cassie—because he'd already broken his promise to her to keep this thing between them strictly no-strings. No emotions. Because he loved her, plain and simple.

That last lethal realization had come out of nowhere, and yet deep down, he knew he'd known it for a while now. Perhaps that's why he'd resisted getting involved with her to begin with. Because it had been so easy to fall.

Cassie looked so soft and beautiful in the ambient light. *So...mine.* His heart revved, and Brock closed his eyes and let his head fall back to the couch. "You need to go."

"I can't," she said, so softly he would've missed it if he wasn't so attuned to her. "I think maybe that's the problem."

Her leg brushed his as she moved closer.

"Brock you are not responsible for everything that happens in the world. You can't control everything. Sometimes people die with no warning. People go away. You get left, abandoned, whether by choice or through no fault of anyone. But that's no reason to lock your heart away forever."

He heard more movement and realized she'd slid off the sofa to kneel on the floor. Then she tugged off one of his shoes. Her position reminded him of their early morning activities and those dark erotic thoughts swarmed his beleaguered mind before he could stop them. "I don't want to talk about it."

"I know." Cassie removed his other shoe, then straightened, resting her forearms on the sofa cushions. "But you're not okay. And I'm not leaving you until you are."

He opened his eyes and stared at her, ashamed to feel his throat tighten. "Cassie. Please. Just go."

"No." She laid her head on his thigh and stroked his other leg with a gentle hand. "I want to help you. Tell me what to do."

When he didn't answer, Cassie started by removing the dangling shot glass from his fingers and setting it on the coffee table beside the empty bottle. Then she stood and pulled Brock up with her so she could hug him. He buried his face in her hair and held on to her hard, swallowing against the lump in his throat.

"You're going to be okay," she whispered.

No. No, he wasn't. But he couldn't admit that, so he took a deep breath. He didn't want her wasting her concern on him. He was the caretaker here, not her.

Then she pulled back and grabbed his hand to lead him down the hall to his bedroom.

Bad idea.

The worst sort of bad idea.

He was a good foot taller than Cassie and weighed at least seventy pounds more than her. He could have easily pulled free, but for whatever reason, he allowed her to lead him along like a lost puppy. Along the way, she turned off the lights. Darkness settled over them. Over him. *In* him. He was about as on edge as he ever remembered being in his life.

And he wanted Cassie.

Needed her.

So badly he ached.

But Brock had never been very good at asking. Not that she'd make him…

Cassie pulled him into his bedroom and nudged the door shut with her foot. "Come here."

"You're shaking," he said as he wrapped his arms around her trembling body.

Her hands glided up his chest to cup his face. "No. Not me," she said gently, her eyes shadowed. "*You're* the one shaking, Brock."

Well, hell. He tried to pull back, but she held tight and refused to budge. "Wait—"

"I need to go—"

"This is *your* house." Cassie slid her fingers into his hair, gentle and soothing as she massaged his scalp. Tender. So were her eyes when she tilted his face down to hers in the dim light. "No one's going anywhere," she said. "You're already right where you need to be."

Then she locked the door and gave him a push that had him falling onto his bed.

He was pretty far gone for her to catch him off guard like that. Brock came up on his elbows, and there Cassie stood in her shimmery top and leggings, looking like everything he'd ever wanted, all sweet and warm and caring. *Too* caring. He didn't want that. It made him feel too raw and vulnerable and special. "I want to be alone."

"You don't need to be alone tonight."

"You don't know what I need."

She stared down at the bulge straining the front of his scrub pants. "I think I have a pretty good idea." She pulled off her top and tossed it on the floor. "Sure you don't want to talk first?"

Sitting up, Brock settled his hands on her rib cage, fingers spread wide.

"It might help if you did," she said.

He took in her pretty pink bra, one that gave him tantalizing peekaboo hints of her nipples, which were already hard. They puckered up even tighter under his gaze, and his mouth watered.

"Brock?"

"Sorry. You with your top off is distracting." He closed his eyes and then stared up at the ceiling. He badly wanted to roll her beneath him and take her. Take her hard and fast and dirty. But he couldn't because it would be against their agreement of no strings, no feelings—at least for him.

"Good," she said, and it took Brock a second to realize she was responding to what he'd said before and not what he was thinking just then. "How about we continue where we left off this morning?" She crawled onto the bed and then over him, letting her stomach brush over his erection. "Seems you like that suggestion."

Through his haze, Brock felt her hands stroke his thighs. Then higher as her fingers deftly untied his scrub pants and tugged them down enough to free him. He warned her, "I'm not in the mood to be teased."

"Who's teasing?" She smiled.

He groaned. *Jesus*. "Cassie—"

"Shh." Her warm breath brushed over him as she wriggled into place between his legs. Brock groaned again.

"I have your attention?" she asked.

"You *always* have my attention. Cassie—"

"No." She grasped him with her hand. "Let me do this for you. Please."

His protest turned into a husky moan when her lips slowly descended over him.

He was lost after that, his hands fisted tightly in the bedding instead of in her hair because he wasn't at all sure he could control himself and be gentle. Just two minutes in, he was drowning in pleasure and hot, desperate need.

"Cassie—" he gasped again, trying to warn her.

She let out a hungry little murmur and hummed her approval around him. Brock came fast and hard and knew he should be mortified. But for now, all he could muster was blissed-out exhaustion...

When he woke several hours later to the alarm, he was alone, leaving him to wonder if he'd dreamed it all.

The next day came too early, and Cassie cursed her alarm. She'd left Brock sprawled out, spread-eagled on his bed—well after 2:00 a.m. with his eyes rolled back in his head—and had returned to the guesthouse.

She got up and peeked out the window to see the driveway empty. He must have left already. She got up and got dressed, had some breakfast, then worked on the details of Serene's surgery, which was coming up the following week.

Later, she got a text from Riley saying that Adi's school had called and Adi fell in a mud puddle and needed a clean set of clothes—socks, shoes, shirt, pants, underwear, coat. Everything. Apparently, the little girl had made quite a mess.

Cassie went to Adi's room and got a new outfit for her, then drove to the elementary school. They'd been right. Adi was a mess, but a happy one.

"I don't need new clothes," the little girl said, unhappy now that she had to change.

"Yeah, you do." Cassie handed Adi the clothes and gave her hair a tousle. Or tried. Her fingers caught on caked dirt, and Cassie wrinkled her nose. "Did you bathe in the mud?"

Adi grinned, and Cassie shook her head. "See you at the bus stop in a little while, sweetie."

She left the school and met Luna and Madison for a late lunch at the Buzzy Bird.

"So sad what happened to Mrs. Preston," Madi said. "We're all taking it hard at the hospital. Especially Brock." Her eyes cut to Cassie. "Have you talked to him?"

Not since I left him boneless and panting on his bed.

Cassie shook her head and shoved a couple of fries in her mouth.

"He might need some TLC," Madi said suggestively.

"Stop it," Luna said, smacking Madi on the arm. "Listen, Cassie. Just do him. That's all the TLC he'll need."

Cassie nearly inhaled her tea. By the time she'd stopped coughing and swiped at her streaming eyes, both Madi and Luna were waiting, brows up.

"Stop it," Cassie managed. "Don't read too much into anything. I'm just staying at his guesthouse. That's all. We're having fun."

"Fun, huh? I bet you are." Luna snorted.

"Yes." *No.* Ugh. It was complicated, at least for Cassie. She'd gone into this whole thing with Brock thinking she had it clear in her head. She'd help him with his daughter and his schedule. They'd have a nice time together. Then it would all be over, and she'd go back to San Diego. She'd thought being with him might get him out of her system once and for all. But somewhere along the way, without her noticing, Brock had gotten under her skin, around her carefully constructed boundaries and rules. With his sexy smile and his sizzling, seductive swagger. Then there was Adi and Winnie. Both of whom she'd come to care for far more than she should. Even Riley had become a friend. She'd thought leaving these people and Wyckford behind again would be easy. Now, she was beginning to see how wrong she'd been.

Cassie wasn't about to tell her friends about that though. Bad enough they, and half the town, were already gossiping about her and Brock. So she cleared her throat and straightened, saying as firmly as possible, "Look, all this is only temporary. Our arrangement. Anything that happens between me and Brock. We've been clear on that from the start. None of this is real. I'll be going back to California after my patient is stable and recovering from the surgery next week."

"But is that what you want?" Madi asked. "Because changing your mind is allowed, Cassie."

"I'm a partner in a very successful practice. One I helped build. Yes, I'm sure," Cassie said with more certainty than she felt presently. "I have patients. I have a life I love. I'm not going to leave all that behind because of some summer fling."

"Is that all it is though?" Madi gave her a far too perceptive stare. "Because from the dreamy look on your face when you walked in here, I'd say it's a bit more than that. I haven't seen you look this way since med school." She reached across the table and patted Cassie's hand. "Look, if this is all just for fun, that's great. Lord knows Brock could use some. And you could too. But please be honest with yourself before you get hurt. You both have lots of things going on—important things—that could create real problems if you're not clear on what you want. And what you want might be different now than when you first arrived."

Cassie had strived hard for the past five years. Always pushing. Always go, go, go. It meant a lot to her, proving her worth, but it'd also cost her. Until now she'd not managed to have any real, lasting romantic relationships in her life. It hadn't been a priority. But now…

"Happiness should always win," Madi said quietly.

Cassie sighed. They ate in companionable silence for a few minutes.

"So on a scale of one to ten," Luna asked, never one to be shy. "How good is he?"

Cassie thought about her and Brock's two extremely memorable…moments. "Definitely an eleven."

"And you're happy." Madi said softly. Not a question.

Cassie looked into her friend's warm brown eyes and was about to say that happiness didn't matter, but that wasn't correct. Not anymore. Not entirely. "I've always been a little short on happy," she admitted. "So it's hard to say. But it doesn't matter. Like I said, all this is temporary."

It didn't feel temporary though, because somehow, when she hadn't been looking, she'd begun to yearn for more.

She'd begun to want permanent.

Which was a huge issue since as far as she knew, Brock hadn't changed his mind about their agreement. He still thought this was an easy, no-strings affair. And he already had more than enough complications on his plate. Cassie didn't want to be another.

Not to mention the logistical nightmares a long-distance relationship would create if they did decide to try out more.

No. Best to leave things as is and take the wonderful memories with them into the future.

Separate futures.

Madi was still watching her far too closely for Cassie's comfort. Her friend had always had a knack for seeing things other people wanted to keep hidden. "You could do this the easy way and just tell him, you know."

"Tell who what?" Luna asked, her gaze darting between the two of them as she frowned.

"That she's falling for him," Madi said.

Cassie shook her head. "What? No. I'm not falling for anyone."

She wasn't. She couldn't be falling in love. Not with Brock. Not with anyone. Because her life was already full and there wasn't any room for romance in it. She'd made that clear. And Brock didn't have time for a relationship either, what with raising Adi on his own and his busy practice. No. There was no falling on either side. They'd agreed. Keep it light and fun.

"You really don't think you're falling for him?" Madi asked again.

Cassie shook her head. And even if she was, she'd get over it. She'd done it before. She'd do it again. Her life since she'd left Wyckford had always been about achievements. It'd never been about emotions, about heart and soul. About falling in love…

Cassie's phone rang. A number she didn't recognize. She answered with a frown.

"Dr. Cassandra Murphy?" came an unfamiliar voice in her ear.

"Yes."

"This is Nancy, I'm the school nurse at Bay Elementary. Riley Turner gave me your number."

"Okay…"

"Adi fell in a mud puddle again…"

* * *

Since there was only a half hour left of school, rather than bring yet another set of clean clothes, Cassie took Adi home this time. After buckling the kid into the booster seat she'd strapped into her rental SUV, Cassie climbed in behind the wheel, shooting Adi a look in the rearview mirror as she pulled out of the parking lot. "Why were you in the puddle again?"

"Camel flaunting," the little girl said seriously. "We needed to camel flaunt."

This baffled Cassie for a beat, then she had to laugh. "Camouflage?"

"Yes," Adi said.

Cassie had never taken the time to really picture herself with kids. She liked them, figured she'd have some one day, but after she'd established herself in her career and moved into her dream home and... There always seemed to be something else on the list to accomplish before she started a family. But in that moment, sharing a grin in the mirror with Adi, something deep inside her squeezed hard in yearning.

They'd just walked in the front door and let Winnie loose when Brock pulled up.

He got out of his car looking like the day had already been too long. "Need my laptop," he growled, eyes shadowed, face drawn. He made time to stop and hug Adi before meeting Cassie's eyes.

She wanted to ask him if he was okay or give him a hug like he'd given his daughter. She wanted to have him in bed again, shuddering with release, her name on his lips as he climaxed.

But mostly she wanted to talk to him about their agreement. To find out if he felt similar to her—that this whole thing might be getting uncomfortably close to being a lot more than just temporary—and if they should continue or call the entire thing off.

"Hey," she said, hating how breathless she sounded.

His gaze searched hers for a long beat, but he gave nothing away. Something else Brock was extremely good at. "Where'd all the mud come from?"

Cassie told him about the puddle and the camel flaunt while Adi went to take a bath. Brock strode into the living room, looking as if he needed a long vacay.

"You okay?" Cassie followed him.

"Don't know." He lifted his head and pinned her with his gaze. "About last night…"

"What about it?" she asked carefully, not wanting to confess anything yet.

He looked at her for another long moment,

then stepped toward her, but his phone went off. Brock swore, grabbed his laptop and strode to the door.

Cassie let out a breath, then sucked it in again as he returned to kiss her quickly. "We'll talk later."

CHAPTER THIRTEEN

It was a long day.

Seemed every patient at the office and his staff wanted to talk about Mrs. Preston. Everyone was devastated. By the time he got home, Brock was more exhausted than he'd been the previous night, and that was saying something.

He'd called ahead. Adi was asleep. Riley was heading back for another shift at the hospital. He'd have the whole house to himself. He could have done whatever he wanted with the evening. But there was only one thing on his agenda to do.

Cassie.

The lights in the guesthouse blazed. Through the windows, Brock saw her sitting on the couch, taking a video call on her computer with other doctors from her practice out in California.

A visceral reminder of her whole other life outside of his.

Her hair was pulled up in a ponytail, but a few

strands had escaped, framing her face, brushing her throat and shoulders. Just looking at her had Brock's body humming. And though she couldn't possibly see him standing in the dark night, Cassie went still, turned her head and peered outside. Unerringly looking right at him.

She said something to the people on her screen, then closed her laptop and rose in one fluid motion. She stepped outside and shut the door behind her.

They met in the shadows near the shallow end of the pool.

"Hey," she said, a vision in her white top and shorts showing a mile of sexy, tanned leg.

"Hey yourself," he said. "How'd your day go?"

"Well, I didn't kill your dog and Adi continues to master the English language. I'd say that's progress."

"Great." Brock shoved his hands in his pockets to keep from reaching for her, rocking back on his heels instead.

She nibbled on her lower lip. "Can we talk now?"

"Sure." He led her over to the chairs beside the pool and they sat down at the small table there.

Cassie took a deep breath. "This thing between us... It's still temporary, right?"

He studied her a moment, trying to read how she was feeling. But she had her guarded, professional expression on now, the one he couldn't decipher. His gut screamed for him to tell her the truth. His logical brain though, urged caution. He went with facts. Facts were good. Facts were black and white. Facts didn't turn on you and break your heart. "That's what we agreed to."

"Right. We did." She blew out a breath and looked away. "I'm sorry. I guess I'm not very good at this. I don't know what to do with a guy like you."

"A guy like me?" Brock asked, frowning, trying to figure out what that meant.

"Look, it's fine. I knew going into this thing that it couldn't possibly work, but I guess I kept…" She broke off then and stared down at her clasped hands on the table. "I'm sorry."

"Sorry?" he repeated. "For what? Cassie I'm trying like hell to follow you but…"

She looked up at him and blinked, as if she didn't understand how he wasn't catching the obvious. "Our lives are different," she said, shrugging. "You've got a whole life here, a thriving practice, a kid. And I'm busting my butt in San Diego, trying to build the next big treatment in reconstructive surgery. I don't see how those two things can ever mix, with all the distance and the time involved and…" She trailed off, looking at him again, as if expecting him to nod in agreement.

But Brock was still clueless. "Okay. First, if you think my life is working on some grand plan I devised," he said, "then you haven't been paying attention. None of this is how I planned. Nothing. After Kylie died, it was a mess. Then my parents were gone, leaving me with no support and a sister who needed care and Adi to raise. Then the practice." He scrubbed a hand over his face. "God, the practice. Most of the time I'm just struggling to keep up with it all."

"And us? What about this thing with us?"

"This was supposed to be fun," he said with grim amusement. "That's what you wanted, right?"

She stared at him. There weren't crickets out tonight, but if there had been, they'd be chirping about now.

They sat there for several beats in silence, then Cassie sat back and peered up at the sky. "Did you know I had a crush on you during residency?"

Brock snorted, then sighed. "Yeah, Kylie mentioned something to me about it. Why?"

Cassie let out a shaky breath. "Well, I also knew how much you loved Kylie and when you guys announced your engagement at the Fourth of July picnic, I knew it was over. So that's when I decided to take the job offer in California…"

"And start a new life," he finished for her.

Brock was starting to get the whole picture now and nodded. Seemed any relationship between them had been doomed a lot longer than just the past few weeks.

"The life I have now is important to me. I worked hard to make something of myself in California. To put the past behind me." Cassie let out a low laugh and looked at him again. "I'm not ready to give that up yet. Especially for something temporary. Does that make sense?"

Her gaze met his, clear and utterly unfathomable. This was it. The moment of truth.

Tell her how you feel. Tell her this isn't just a fling for you. Tell her…

But five years of struggle and heartache and constant low-level grief had taken its toll on him, and he just couldn't. Couldn't put himself out there like that again—not unless he was sure.

"Understood," he said slowly.

She nodded. Her expression held a hint of something Brock couldn't quite place—disappointment, maybe? Or resignation perhaps. "Good. I wanted to get that out there because I know you're the type to feel responsible for those who cross your path. You're a rescuer."

Okay, now Brock was getting pissed. Cassie

didn't want him to care. He got that, loud and clear. He didn't want to care either. But he did, dammit.

"Look, Cassie. Yes, this thing between us is temporary. That's what we agreed to. But that doesn't give you the right to start psychoanalyzing my life and thinking you know what's going on with me."

She watched him closely, then slowly nodded. "You're right. I'm sorry."

Cassie stood and started back toward the guesthouse, and Brock grimaced. He was screwing all this up big time.

"Wait—"

"Adi lost a tooth tonight," Cassie said as she stopped on the path and looked back at him over her shoulder. "She was excited and wanted to wait up for the tooth fairy but didn't make it. The fairy arrived the minute after she'd conked out."

He reached for his wallet without thinking. "Thanks. How much—"

"Don't worry about it. I got it covered." With that, Cassie let herself into the guesthouse and shut the door quietly.

Brock stood there a moment longer, then returned to his house. That conversation had not gone as he'd wanted it to. Rather than getting any clarity on their situation, he felt like she'd lanced him alive.

Inside her room, he found his daughter deeply asleep, wrapped around Winnie and holding Lola. The book was there too, with the family on the cover displayed prominently.

Brock ignored the pain in his chest, the one that said he was failing the people in his life, as always, and gently pulled the toy from Adi's slack grip and set it on its charging stand. Next, he eyed the dog.

Winnie opened one eye and gave him a look that said, *Don't even try, pal.*

Brock gave up and covered them both.

Winnie licked his hand.

He bent over his daughter and kissed her temple. She smelled like peanut butter and soap, which he took as a good sign. Adi smiled in her sleep, showing him the new, gaping hole in the front.

"Love you, Adi-bean," Brock whispered, the words a heavy weight on his chest.

His daughter rolled away, pulling the dog under one arm and the book under the other, sighing softly in her sleep.

The next morning, Cassie returned to Sunny Village to see her dad. They were back in the art studio, with a new model up on the pedestal today. This woman was artfully draped in a sheet, supposedly like a Grecian goddess, though to Cassie she looked more toga party.

"I wouldn't mind being twenty years younger, like you, Cassie," Mrs. Gregory, the woman seated next to her father, said. "Back to when my body looked as good as yours."

"You mean *fifty* years," her dad murmured, full of snark.

Cassie ignored the conversation and counted down the last twenty minutes of class. Drawing was not her forte, but she was doing it to spend more time with her dad. Her sketch resembled more of an abstract bush than a human body, but it was what it was. After this, she had another call with her practice about the surgery to put the finishing tweaks on the procedure. Then next week, this would all be over. She'd go back to California and life in Wyckford would continue without her. Images of Brock and Adi going through their daily routines, Madi and Luna laughing and falling in love, her father running the retirement home like his own personal kingdom...

It all made her heart ache.

She sighed and stared at her attempt to sketch the angle of the model's hand in the air, but it looked more like a lopsided potato. Brock's housekeeper was back this week too. She'd met Lois, the small Italian woman, earlier that morning and explained that she was staying in the guesthouse. The woman had looked at Cassie with suspicion, but then went about her business. So yeah. Brock's house would be clean and tended to. She did worry about who would take care of Adi though. And Brock for that matter. He'd yet to replace the nanny who'd left shortly after Cassie's arrival, and if he didn't find someone soon, it could leave them in a bind after the surgery when she left for home.

Cassie shook her head and leaned back to squint at her ugly picture. She was being silly. Brock was a grown man. Perfectly capable of taking care of himself, not to mention everyone around him. He'd proven that by managing more than the average human should ever have to— between his practice, the ER, Adi, Riley…the loss of his beloved wife and his parents.

And yes, it was one of the things about him that Cassie found most appealing: his caring, protective nature. But it would be nice for him realize it was okay to be on the other side of the fence occasionally and let someone else do the caring and protecting.

"And that's time," Ben called out to the class.

Cassie kissed her dad's cheek, then grabbed her purse and headed to the door. "Gotta go."

"Hold on," Ben said, pulling a bottle of wine from beneath his bench and handing it to Cassie.

"What's this for?" She frowned. "I'm not much of a drinker—"

"Check out the label."

It was a color pencil sketch of the Wyckford pier at night, lit up with strings of white lights that glowed out over the bay beneath a full moon. She'd seen the original when Luna had sold the drawing to the winery a month ago. When she recognized it, she grinned, filled with pride for her friend's talent. "It's beautiful."

"Thought you might like to have one as a souvenir," her dad told her. "Or maybe you can open it during a nice romantic dinner with Brock."

Cheeks hot, Cassie stuffed the bottle in her bag and avoided his gaze. "We're not having a romance, Dad. Listen, I know you're like the gossip guru in town, but there's nothing between Brock and me."

Ben smiled. "Are you sure?"

"Absolutely," Cassie said firmly, ignoring the little ping inside her. She'd gotten zero feedback emotionally from Brock last night during their talk, and now she thought maybe that was an answer itself. "I'm helping him out with his daughter and we're working on a case together. In exchange, he's letting me use his guesthouse. That's it."

Everyone's ears perked up at this.

Cassie hightailed it out of there and drove to

Brock's, where she waited for the bus. When Adi hopped off it, the little girl was bouncing up and down with excitement. It was Back-to-School Night, and later Brock would get to see Adi receive the Student of the Week award. He'd promised her an ice-cream sundae afterward, then Adi was having her first sleepover at a friend's house.

Adi was so excited that she could hardly contain herself. They walked the half block home, where Cassie let the dog and Adi run wild laps around the yard until they expelled enough energy to sit quietly while Adi did her homework and Cassie worked on Winnie's so-called obedience. This was more an exercise in patience than anything else, but she was determined.

They had mac and cheese and turkey hot dogs for an early dinner—following the dietary restriction cards to a T—then waited for Brock to arrive to take Adi to Back-to-School Night.

Except he didn't show.

Cassie called his cell but got no answer. She tried Riley next. No answer there either. Finally, she drove Adi to the elementary school herself, steamed at everyone with the last name Turner except for Adi.

Adi's teacher seemed thrilled to see her. "Sadie had her kittens. Want to go look?"

When the little girl whooped and raced off,

Cassie looked at the teacher. "How much time before the awards?"

"At least half an hour."

"Can I leave Adi here while I find her father?" Cassie asked.

"Dr. Turner?"

"Yes. I'm guessing he got hung up with a patient…"

The teacher nodded and Cassie hurried back to her car.

Brock's office was in a building directly adjacent to the hospital. She tore into the lot, hurried to his office and yanked open the front door. Righteous anger bloomed within her, propelling her forward, ready to tear him a new one for missing something so important to Adi.

Underneath it though, something else was blooming too.

Worry.

This wasn't like Brock. He never blew off anything that anyone needed, but especially Adi. His daughter came first with him. Family always came first. So this bothered Cassie. She hadn't expected to feel worried for the man who'd occupied her fantasies for the last five years. Hell, she hadn't meant to feel anything for him at all, but she did.

Far too much.

The waiting room was empty. The front office area was lit but also empty. Cassie's anxiety amped up a notch.

"Brock?" she called, walking down the hallway.

At the end of the corridor, she came to a partially closed door behind which was a large private office decorated in masculine dark wood, the huge mahogany desk loaded with paperwork and files. The lights were on, and there was a mug of something on the corner next to an open laptop.

Behind the desk was a large executive chair. In it was Brock, leaning back, feet up.

Fast asleep.

CHAPTER FOURTEEN

BROCK HATED FALLING asleep in his office chair. It always gave him a kink in his neck and made him grumpy as hell. So, when he leaned back and let his eyes drift shut, he told himself he was merely resting his eyelids.

"Brock?"

That voice, Cassie's voice, drifted to him on a breath of air, and he relaxed into his seat.

His hands went to her hips to pull her in closer, needing her so badly but he refused to rush. If this was all they were going to have, which according to their conversation the previous night it was, then he wanted it to last. He kissed her neck, tracing his tongue over the sensitive spot just below her ear, eliciting the sweetest sigh he'd ever heard. This fueled a bone-deep desire to mark Cassie as his, and he sucked the patch of skin into his mouth.

"Brock…"

No. No talking, or this would end. He slipped

his hands beneath the hem of her top, feeling all that smooth soft skin, and groaned.

"*Brock,*" the voice said again, more persistent.

In response, he grabbed her wrist and tugged so Cassie fell into his lap with a gasp that had him opening his eyes and realizing it wasn't a dream at all...

Oh, God.

"Sorry," she said, wriggling to free herself from his hold. "I didn't mean to startle you."

Residency had taught Brock how to sleep light and awaken fast, but apparently, he'd forgotten the art of both. Then again, certain parts of him were *very* awake now, and getting more so by the second thanks to Cassie's squirming.

Her eyes widened at the feel of him beneath her. "Um..."

"Yeah," he said thickly. "Sit still a minute, please."

She met his gaze and blushed at whatever she saw there.

The air crackled around them.

"Not that I'm *not* enjoying you on my lap," he said, "but why are you here? And where's Adi?"

Cassie gave him a look that screamed he wasn't as alert as he'd thought. "It's Back-to-School Night and you're late. You weren't answering your cell, so I came looking for you."

"Damn." Brock stood fast and set Cassie aside, wishing this could've lasted longer.

But his daughter was waiting, and Brock couldn't believe he'd fallen asleep like that. Then again, after another eighty-plus hour work week, maybe he could believe it. He shut his laptop, grabbed his keys and his phone and tugged Cassie after him out the door. Then he stopped and looked down into her concerned face. She'd come to get him because she cared about Adi.

Did that mean she might care about him too?

He felt eviscerated by how much he wanted that to be true. Needed that to be true.

It had been so long since someone had cared about him like that. Like Kylie had loved him, cared for him. Adi loved him, of course, but that was different. Tate, Mark... Hell, even his sister, though he wouldn't bet against the house on that one.

His patients and staff liked him too. But maybe it was time to step back, to not take the weight of the world on his shoulders. To let a little bit of that control slip from his fingers since it really was all an illusion anyway.

"Brock?" Cassie asked. "Are you okay?"

"Not yet, but I will be."

He knew he needed to come to a decision. It had been brewing for a while now. It was hard, probably the hardest of his life so far, but necessary all the same. Tomorrow, he planned to come back here—to his office on a Saturday, when the practice was closed—and mull it all over. It was time. More than time. He had to devise a workable plan for himself, for Adi, for everyone. And Brock needed to do what was right for his patients too. He'd loved his dad, loved the memory of his dad right here in this office, helping people.

But it was no longer as relevant as making his own life work. And maybe, just maybe, if he sat down and came up with a plan to make his personal life work, it would prove to Cassie that there was a chance for them to work too. As more than a fling. As more than temporary.

They were still in the hallway, and she was staring at him very solemnly. "What's wrong? What's happening here?"

Brock didn't really have words for how he felt about his decision yet. His world was a little off center now, like he was standing at the edge of a cliff with one foot in the air already. It was a new feeling for him, this uncertainty. He hadn't done anything yet. There was still tonight for him to think on it, to consider all his options. But normally, once he'd made up his mind, he didn't go back.

"Nothing yet," he said, because it was true. Also, Cassie stood so close, looking so cute and effortlessly sexy, that he backed her up to the wall with his body.

"Brock," she said as her hands went to his chest. "We need to get to the school."

He pressed into her slightly, feeling a little warm. Feeling a lot of things actually. "I know."

Her brow creased more tightly in that adorable expression of concern. "We need to go."

"Yep." He slid a hand down her back to her very nice ass and rocked her into him. She was right. There was no time now. But that was going to change.

Or so he hoped.

Too bad he had no guarantee she'd want more, would stay for more. Still, a man could hope. Leaning in, he kissed her, soft and light, then pulled back. "Let's go see Adi."

They made it to the school in time to see his daughter get her Student of the Week award. Cassie watched Adi beam with happiness at her father and felt her own heart clench. Brock's expression was much more subdued but no less genuine, and Cassie's heart kicked again.

Afterward, she returned to the guesthouse to give them some alone time. As soon as Cassie changed and settled onto the sofa with her phone, a text popped up from Madi with a photo attached. This one had been taken by someone inside the elementary school's kinder-garten classroom. Adi was up on the makeshift stage, accepting her award.

The class was full of proud, smiling parents.

And in the back of the room stood Cassie, beaming at the stage, a flush on her cheeks as Brock stood behind her, his arms around her waist, his jaw pressed to her temple as he also looked toward the stage. There was something about their stance, their body language, the way the air practically shimmered between them.

Or maybe she was reading too much into it. It had been packed in that classroom. There'd been little room to move. They'd stood that way to conserve space.

Or not.

Something tightened deep inside Cassie then, something strong and warm and lasting, but she couldn't decide if it was good or bad.

Liar.

It was both. Good because it meant that at long last, she'd finally fallen in love.

Bad because it was with the last person on earth she could be with long-term.

CHAPTER FIFTEEN

MUCH LATER THAT NIGHT, Cassie was lying in bed. The sheets were soft, and she could tell Lois had washed them in the same detergent she used for Brock's from the scent. And when Cassie found herself pressing her face to them instead of sleeping, she got up and strode to the windows.

The night was hot and humid. The lights in the big house were off. Adi was at her friend's house for the sleepover, and Riley was working again. She had no idea where Brock was; either he was out, or he was sleeping.

In front of her, the pool gleamed, the underwater lights making the water glow invitingly. Seeing as how her time here was limited, Cassie decided to go for it. She stripped out of her camisole and panties and pulled on a bathing suit. She'd go for a quick swim to cool off, then maybe she could sleep. To help her relax, she also grabbed the bottle of wine her dad had given her the other day. There was a corkscrew in the kitchen but no wineglasses. No problem. She took the entire bottle outside, where she sat on the edge of the pool and dangled her feet in the water.

Heaven.

She watched the moon and stars and sipped wine for a while, wondering if this counted as fun too. It felt decadent and different from the time she and Brock spent together. But yeah. Still fun.

Cassie took another sip of the wine, set the bottle at her hip, then slipped into the pool with hardly a ripple.

The cool water on her heated skin felt so good as she dived deep. The delicious rush of it over her instantly brought down her body temp. She swam a few laps, then lazily floated to the far side of the pool, leaned on the edge and kicked gently, looking out at the rising moon before swimming across once more to sip more wine. Eventually a light came on in the main house and soon her dreamy haze was interrupted by a splash at the other end of the pool. Then Brock was there, emerging at her side.

Her heart stopped, starting again when he leaned close, the heat of him enveloping her even as the chlorine-scented water rushed off his face and shoulders. He was tall enough to stand here where she couldn't, the water hitting him midchest.

Their eyes met. His lashes were wet and spiky, his blue eyes dark and deep and intense. He didn't speak, and neither did she. Reaching out, he stroked the wet hair at her temple, drawing his finger slowly down her cheek to the corner of her mouth, his gaze following the movement.

She shivered. "Brock—"

"Shh." He put a finger over her lips, pausing for a beat before lowering his face to hers. Replacing his finger with his mouth, his tongue traced the line of her lower lip.

She moaned, low and throaty as his hands slid up her back. Using the water's momentum to curl into his chest, she fell into him willingly. He nuzzled her neck, his lips warm against her now-chilled skin, and she sucked in a breath.

Lifting his head, he met her gaze. His fingers cradled her head as he ran his lips along her jawline to her neck. His tongue was right there, on the vulnerable spot beneath her ear, and just like that, he had her.

Whatever he wanted… Cassie would give him. Because she wanted it too.

He kissed her, slow and hungry and powerful, and the night—the moon, the stars, everything—spun around her. Brock deepened the kiss, turning it into a second one, then a third, then so many more that she lost count, his warm hands cupping her breasts, caressing her nipples.

She realized he'd untied and removed her bikini top without her even noticing.

Brock raised his head, and Cassie arched into him in the moonlight, wanting him to touch her, wanting his mouth on her.

But he just looked at her, and she couldn't tell what he was thinking. It was excruciating. It was exciting. It was exquisitely, impossibly sexy. Needing more liquid courage to endure this, Cassie reached for the wine bottle, but Brock took it gently from her. Watching her intently, he sipped from the bottle, and again, drinking more deeply.

She couldn't take her eyes off him, the way the sleek muscles of his throat worked as he swallowed.

Finally, he set the bottle aside and kissed her again. His mouth was sweet from the wine, and fiery desire flamed through her—through him too, based on the groan rumbling up from his chest. Lifting her up, Brock took one of Cassie's nipples into his mouth, his fingers dancing down her spine. Everything he did felt so sensual, so slow and dreamlike.

She nearly went over the edge right then and there. One more touch and she might have too, but then his eyes met hers, unreadable, showing nothing but a reflection of the moon.

Nothing of the man inside.

She wanted, needed, to know how she affected him and if he cared at all. About her, about this night, about the future. If he was as desperate for her as she was for him. She slid her hands up his taut abs and to his chest, humming in pleasure at the feel of all those firm muscles. It wasn't enough. She needed more. "Brock…"

Brock kissed her throat, her collarbone, her shoulders. His fingers trailed down her belly and caressed her through the fabric of her bikini bottom. Then he slid the material aside and his fingers touched her, dipping inside her as he kissed her deeply.

Cassie pressed tight to him, loving the feel of his hard, wet body against hers. He *was* hard, and she palmed him gently, using her thumb to tease him. His hips jerked into her touch, and he kissed her harder, his mouth searing.

"Out of the pool," he finally said, his voice low and commanding. He vaulted himself out of the water in one easy movement, then reached back to pull her out too, with no effort at all. "Come on."

She had no idea where they were going and didn't care.

* * *

Brock pulled a wet Cassie in close. Her skin felt like velvet against his, and her breath warm against his throat. Even though so much was up in the air between them, he was sure of one thing: they were finally doing this.

He kissed her again, swift and rough, and she moaned and clutched at him eagerly.

"I need you, Brock," she whispered. "Please."

Hell yeah. He pulled back and eyed their surroundings. He had two plush lounge chairs only a few feet away, beneath the terrace, protected by the bushes he'd yet to prune back for the year.

Perfect.

He took Cassie over to one, nudged her onto it, then followed her down. He kissed her lips, long and hard, leaving them swollen and wet as he shifted down toward her breasts again. He laved one nipple, loving how Cassie gasped and those little panting whimpers that fueled his lust to the point of no return. Common sense said he should stop this and get them inside but screw it. He didn't want to move. The cool air, her hot body beneath his, her hands touching him everywhere she could reach—it all felt amazing. He slid a hand to the small of her back, then to her ass, tilting her so the heat between her legs rubbed his thigh as she rocked her hips. They were still a mystery to each other outside of this, but here he knew what she needed. Mouth on hers, he set a rhythm, and her legs tightened on him like a vise.

"*Brock*." Her nails dug into his biceps, her breathing heavy. *Close*, he thought, *so close*, and then Cassie tore her mouth from his. "Oh, God. I'm going to—"

"Yes, let go for me, darling."

She burst into wild shudders in his arms. Brock held her and watched as she rode out the waves of pleasure. It was the sexiest thing he'd ever seen.

When she finally relaxed, Cassie tugged him down on top of her. "Tell me you have a condom tonight."

He laughed. "In my pocket."

This caused some trouble since his shorts were still drenched from the pool, but she managed to get her fingers on the sealed foil packet when he sat up a little to remove his. Shorts completely. She insisted on doing the honors herself, which meant by the time she'd rolled the condom down his length, he quivered with need.

"Now," Cassie said, and guided him home.

The hot, tight, wet heat of her felt so good. Then she arched her hips, and Brock saw fireworks. "Cassie," he whispered hoarsely, nipping at her jaw. "Slow down."

"Later."

Things had gotten completely out of his control here, and damn if he didn't love it. Love her. Already breathing crazily, he set his forehead to Cassie's and began to move within her as she rocked against him.

"Please," she whispered, her fingers in his hair, her body straining and moving with his in a way that took him straight to the brink all too soon. Everything in him tightened as he barreled like a runaway train to the end of the line. "Cassie. Don't move."

But, of course, she kept moving. His fingers dug into her hips, and there was no hope of reining her in. He didn't even try. She drew him deeper into her body, and she buried herself deeper into his heart and soul.

When she cupped his face and looked up at him, letting him see everything as she burst again, it was his undoing. He hurtled over the edge along with her, thrusting hard into her one last time before collapsing over her in a boneless heap. Brock tried to move, to pull back, but Cassie wouldn't let him, her arms and legs wrapped tight around him, keeping him in place. Finally, she allowed him to shift his hands from her ass to the lounge chair to support his own weight again.

He withdrew and dealt with the condom, then laid back down beside her, curling her naked body into his, spoon-style. They remained like that for a few long moments, breathing the same air, their legs entangled. It was the most perfect moment he could remember in a long time, and Brock planned to rewind and repeat the entire experience. Just as soon as he recovered.

Cassie snuggled up in a big, warm, sated Brock, thinking she'd never felt so amazing. She'd just started to doze off when his cell phone rang on the table nearby.

Crap.

She stirred enough to whisper over her shoulder, "Someone's trying to get a hold of you."

Brock grunted. "They always are."

The night was dark with only a sliver of a moon. After a final lingering kiss, he got up and pulled on his shorts, then dived into the pool's depths to find Cassie's bikini. Once he'd retrieved it, he helped her into it, tying the straps at her back and neck while she dealt with the bottoms. Good thing he helped her make sure everything was back in place because she was pretty much a bowl of jelly. Then he grabbed his phone and hit redial.

"Well?" Cassie asked when he'd hung up.

"It's Adi. She just wants to come home." His gaze met hers. "Cassie—"

"If you're going to say you're sorry, please

don't. Or if you regret this, or if it was just plain awful and—"

He shut her up with another kiss. When they ran out of air, he pulled back and smiled. "I was going to thank you. This was wonderful. And thank you for finding me."

It took her a moment to realize he was talking about her coming to his office earlier. What he hadn't said though was anything about their situation. Then again, maybe he'd said it all already. Sex wasn't the same for men as it was for women; she knew that. But still, this had felt different. Deeper. More meaningful. At least for her...

She reached up and cupped his jaw. "I'll always find you."

He brought her hand to his mouth and kissed her palm, giving her a quizzical look. "Not sure what that means, but can you hold that thought until tomorrow? I need to go pick up my daughter."

She sighed and smiled. Hold that thought. The story of their lives. Cassie kissed him once more, quickly, then stepped back. "Go. Get Adi. And be careful."

"Always." He smiled back, then kissed her. "'Night, Cassie."

"'Night."

CHAPTER SIXTEEN

BROCK WENT THROUGH several straight days of craziness at work. The amazing night with Cassie had resulted in an even more amazing weekend together, with him having a couple rare days off. They'd stayed around the house, playing games with Adi, talking, cooking, going over the surgery this week and making love at night. It had been lovely. The closeness, the sweetness, the support.

He could almost imagine a life where his schedule matched that every day. He'd even gone into his office for a while on Saturday and sat there alone, running the numbers. Setting aside his emotions surrounding the sale of the practice, it really did seem like the best solution. He could still stay on there, still see his patients, still make sure that it all ran to his dad's high expectations. He'd even decided to have his attorney add a clause into the hospital's contract that he got veto power over any decisions made regarding layoffs, staffing changes, and patient care initiatives. If they agreed to his demands, then yes. He'd sign the contract. He'd stay on and begin searching for another GP to join him in caring for the people of Wyckford. He'd get on that first thing Monday morning.

Life would be good again... even better if Cassie stayed.

He quickly silenced that voice. Even though they'd been pretty much inseparable for the last seventy-two hours, there were still things left unsaid between them. Mainly the fact that Brock was in love with Cassie and Cassie was still going home to California sooner rather than later.

That last thought continued to chase around the inside of his head as Monday arrived. Despite getting in early, there'd been no time to deal with the contract as he'd wanted. Instead, he'd seen four flu sufferers, three routine physicals, two cases of strep and a partridge in a pear tree. By the time he'd had a spare minute to sit down and open his computer, his old doubts around Cassie took precedence. If she decided to stay in Wyckford, it would need to be her decision, not because he'd asked her to. He knew her too well, how hard she'd worked, how good she was at her job. He could never ask her to give that all up for him. And while the medical community in town was becoming bigger every day, it was by no means anything close to the size of San Diego. She shouldn't have to downsize just to be with him.

In fact, he was still thinking about their situation on his drive home that night. That and perhaps getting Cassie alone in the pool again. Except when he walked into his house at a quarter past nine that night, his eyes were gritty with exhaustion, and he thought maybe should lie down for a while and sleep for the rest of his life.

I'll get it all taken care of tomorrow, Brock told himself. Tomorrow he wouldn't be too tired to give something more to the people in his life. Tomorrow he would talk to Cassie about the practice. Tomorrow…

But the next day, the whole town of Wyckford basically shut down early for the summer Bay Festival, an annual event featuring music, food and booths from the local merchants. Brock had promised Madi he'd put in an hour at the free clinic booth after office hours, making nice and taking blood pressure readings for the passersby. So that's where he headed.

In exchange, Madi had arranged for a babysitter for Adi. Thanks to the teen center she ran as a part of the clinic, she had lots of money-hungry teenagers at her disposal, and she'd lined him up with a girl from the local high school.

Adi loved her.

So, with his daughter's care squared away, Brock arrived at the pier. The hot, humid morning had turned into a hot, sultry late afternoon, and he rolled up his sleeves as he walked through the sticky Buzzards Bay air. He spent an hour in the booth, taking the blood pressure of every senior citizen in Wyckford. When it was Ben's turn, the man winked when Brock suggested his blood pressure was a little too high and that Ben needed to slow down some.

"I'll slow down when I'm dead," Ben said, waving in the rest of Sunny Village's blue-haired posse for their turn. Mrs. Tyler asked how Brock felt about cougars, and he really hoped she meant the kind in the wild.

Mrs. Munson grabbed his ass.

Mrs. Dawson asked him for a breast exam.

Brock thought about moving to Tahiti and living on a deserted island.

By the time the sun sank into Buzzards Bay, the festival had kicked into high gear. Brock sat on the pier near the dance floor and thought about the situation with Cassie some more, since she was pretty much top of his mind these days.

Two days from now was Serene's big surgery. They'd spent hours planning and prepping and going over every detail of things to make sure they were perfectly in sync. The custom prosthetics had arrived, and Cassie had taken them to the hospital herself. She'd also coordinated a team of people from radiology and neurology and various maxillofacial specialties to be there on Thursday to make sure everything they could get done that day for Serene would get done. Even Brock's sister had been roped into the team. He had to be impressed by Cassie's masterful leadership of the whole thing. It was a thing of beauty, really. He almost hated for it to be over.

No. There was no "almost" about it. He hated that after the surgery was done and Serene was on the road to recovery, Cassie would leave. It was selfish, he knew, but Brock couldn't help it.

And what will I do afterward?

He shook his head and stared down into the dark waters of the bay. Well, he'd deal with it, he supposed. Pick up the pieces and go on. Same as he had after he'd lost Kylie. Same as he had after he'd lost his parents. Because he had no choice in the matter. Adi needed him. His patients needed him.

If only Cassie needed me too...

For now, he sat back and watched her dancing with her friends. She moved so gracefully and easily to the music that Brock wished time would stop. She wore a lacy camisole top, showing off her lean, toned arms. Her skirt was short, blowing his brain cells right and left. Her strappy sandals made her bare legs look long and sleek. Brock pushed to his feet and met Cassie on the edge of the dance floor.

She smiled. "You dance?"

He gave her a boogie move that made her laugh.

"Wow," she said.

Shaking his head, he pulled her into him as the music slowed. Cassie fit his body like the last pieces of a puzzle, and Brock relaxed for the first time all day. She had one arm around his neck, her fingers playing in his hair, making him want to purr like a big cat. "Sweet."

"Yeah." She nudged closer. *"Sweet..."*

She laughed softly when he tightened his grip on her. He had a hand low on her back, itching to go lower. He'd been thinking about getting his hands on her all day.

Another couple bumped into them. Ben and Mrs. Wartinski. She was ninety, but still had all her own teeth and a driver's license. Ben winked at Brock. "Nice night for romance, eh?"

Brock met Cassie's gaze as the music shifted again, gearing up for a faster-paced song, with their agreement screaming in his head. No romance. No strings. No emotions. Well, Brock had already completely blown those rules where Cassie was concerned. Trouble was, he had no idea where she stood with them. All around them people danced, laughed, talked and drank, which meant this was hardly the place for a serious conversation.

He took Cassie's hand and led her off the dance floor and over to the bar. They got a couple of longnecks and then walked hand in hand down the pier. Instead of going to the end, where they'd be highlighted as if they were in a fishbowl, he directed her to the wood stairs that led down to the beach.

The sand was damp and giving, the water pounding the shore hard enough to drown out most of the sounds of the festival as they walked and sipped their beers. It'd been a long couple of weeks, months, years. Full of irrevocable changes. Brock had made a lot of mistakes in his life, and he'd tried to learn from all of them and not repeat them. Like calculating your risks before rushing headlong into something that might not work out the way you wanted. He needed to know how Cassie felt about this thing between them, if her feelings had changed, but he also didn't want to ruin what little time they might have left together. So he approached the subject neutrally, giving them both a way out, if needed. "Have you set a date yet for your flight back to California?"

"Not yet. I want to make sure Serene is healing properly first." A beat or two passed as they walked on, her hand warm and soft in his. "My colleagues at the practice are already chomping at the bit to get me back."

"I bet," he said, noticing he wasn't the only one who sounded carefully cautious. Cassie's face was averted, and Brock stopped to tilt her face up to his with a finger under her chin, his eyes searching hers. One of them had to be brave. "Is that what you want?"

"I have patients waiting for me," she said. Her gaze was unguarded, letting him see her hopes and dreams and doubts and fears. It was the last that got him. They were at the proverbial fork in the road. "I have a life out there, Brock. One I love. One I worked hard to build."

"I know." His chest constricted, making it hard to breathe.

Tell her. Ask her to stay.

"What about us?"

She pulled away, walking a few steps forward to stare out at the water. "What about us, Brock? These past few weeks have been great. Being with you. Getting to know you and Adi. But that's not real."

"Feels real to me." He hadn't meant to say that aloud, but now it was out there, hanging between them. Buzzards Bay continued to batter the shore. The silence grew taut as they both stared toward the far horizon. Finally, Cassie sighed and looked over at him.

"You barely have time for your life now. That wouldn't change if I moved back."

"It might." His throat tightened as he turned to face her. "If I sell the practice, I'd have more time. For you. For Adi."

"You don't want to do that."

"You don't know what I want, Cassie."

"I helped her with her homework earlier, you know," Cassie said, crossing her arms as if shielding herself. "The family tree thing." She paused. "Kylie was such a great person, Brock. I wish Adi could've known her better."

"Me too." He sighed and frowned. "But what does that have to do with us?"

"Because she needs a mom. I'm not sure if I'm ready for that."

"You'd be great at it," he said, shoving his free hand in his pocket to keep from pulling Cassie into his arms. "She's already crazy about you."

"I know she is. Adi's a great kid. You've done amazing with her." Cassie exhaled slowly. "But the last thing she needs in her life is someone else she cares about to walk away. That's exactly the warning you gave me when we started all this Brock. I don't want to hurt her. Or you."

The "but" in her words hit him like a sucker punch to the gut. *But I can't stay. But I don't*

*love you. But I will be saying good-bye in just
a few days.*

Well, at least now he knew.

Still a bit stunned, Brock slipped his arm
around Cassie's shoulders as they stood on the
shore. This rawness felt familiar, like the same
old grief he'd dealt with for years. A deep, dark
pit that he was getting pretty damn tired of
crawling out of. This time though, he had no
one to blame but himself. Before it had been
the terror of raising a baby on his own, of dealing with Riley's injuries and her mental trauma
because of them, of burying his parents and his
only support system. Now, it was heartache of
a different kind, but no less painful.

Cassie was quiet a moment, then she whispered, "I'm sorry."

He smiled, rubbing his jaw against her hair,
loving her even as his heart shattered. "Not your
fault. Sometimes things just don't work out."

"I know how hard it is for you," she said, snuggling her face into his neck. "My dad worked
so hard to keep food on the table and raise me
by himself after my mom died. Just don't forget
that Adi needs you as much as she does a roof
over her head."

Brock closed his eyes and steeled his resolve.
If they only had a short time left together, he
didn't want to ruin it by becoming maudlin.

They'd agreed. He'd gone into this knowing the score. He'd walk away at the end, just like he'd promised. When he opened his eyes again, he forced a smile and slid his hand down her spine.

She smiled up at him, belying the sadness in her eyes. Hell, if this woman didn't turn him completely upside down and sideways.

Brock nodded, memorizing every little detail of her, before taking Cassie's hand and heading for the pier once more.

CHAPTER SEVENTEEN

CASSIE FELT AWFUL, like something precious, something that might never come again, had slipped away before her eyes. But she hadn't expected Brock to ask her about her feelings like that. She hadn't known what to say. All her life, she'd done what was expected, taken the "right" path.

This trip back to Wyckford was supposed to be just a quick visit, a quick consultation, then back to reality. But it had turned out very differently. And now she wasn't sure what to do. She'd meant what she'd told him. About Adi. About her life in California. About everything.

But you left out the most important thing...

Yes, she loved him. Always had, always would. But her staying wouldn't make anything magically better. He'd still be overworked and under-supported at home. There'd still be the lingering hurt of all he'd lost and all that would never be again. She was a great doctor, but not even she could heal that kind of wound. And the thing was, Brock loved what he did. He was an amazing doctor. His practice thrived because of him. She couldn't ask him to give that up any more than he could ask her to give up hers. So where did that leave them?

Exactly nowhere.

On the way back to the pier, they were stopped multiple times by people wanting to tell Brock their ailments. Everyone wanted to talk to him, to let him know their throat hurt, or they were feeling better, or they planned on calling his office for an appointment next week. She still marveled at how he kept track of it all in his head. Everyone's various ailments and quirks and needs. She needed a laptop and expensive software programs to track all that for her.

But then, that was just Brock. Always thoughtful, always concerned and always giving, to the point he had nothing left for himself.

Cassie was still contemplating all that as they threw their empty bottles away in the recycle bin then climbed the steps back up to the pier, where her father was waiting for them.

Ben Murphy was out of breath as he told them, "A couple of young guys were messing around on the pier, and one fell in. He hasn't surfaced. They're looking for him but—"

Brock was already running toward the small

crowd gathering at the end of the pier, calling back to Cassie. "Call 911."

She did, then quickly followed her dad down the steps on the other side of the pier to the water, anxious to know if the missing guy had been found. An almost hushed crowd was gathered on the rocky beach about a hundred feet away, and they headed there, going as fast as her father could move.

Huddled in the water were three people making their way toward shore, a fourth figure carefully supported between them. Brock and the others staggered ashore, then he dropped to his knees, situating the victim between them, careful with the man's neck and spine.

"Oh, thank God. They found him," Ben huffed out a breath. "I just hope they were in time. Seen more than a couple men drown during my fishing days."

The other men crouched on the opposite side of the unconscious man, water streaming off of all of them. Cassie recognized one of them as flight paramedic Tate Griffin. The other was Samuel Perkins, the neurosurgeon helping her with Serene's case at Wyckford General. He was on his phone, probably talking to the EMS dispatcher or the ER. Brock checked for a pulse and must've found one because he nodded to

Tate before beginning chest compressions, his movements quick and efficient.

"He's not breathing," Cassie said to her father. "That's not good."

There was blood on the man's forehead as well, suggesting a possible head injury. Cassie kicked off her shoes and hurried over to kneel in the sand beside Brock. "What can I do?"

"Check him for any fractures or internal bleeding," Brock said between chest compressions. "Ambulance is on the way."

Carefully, Cassie palpated the man's limbs and thankfully found no signs of broken bones. There was, however, an egg-sized lump on the man's head and a rapidly purpling bruise near his temple.

Just as Brock stopped doing CPR to check for a heartbeat and pulse again, sirens screeched and red-and-blue flashing lights lit up the night as EMS pulled into the lot atop the cliffs above.

Then, an even more welcome sound—the man they were working on choked up seawater, convulsing with the violence of it as his muscles contracted.

Sam and Tate let out audible breaths of relief. Sam stood and pushed the crowd back. Tate accepted several jackets from people standing near, using them to cover the injured man, who now shivered from shock.

Brock deftly turned the man on his side to help him more effectively cough up what looked like gallons of water. As the paramedics ran down the stairs and hit the beach, the man tried to push himself up, but Brock held him down, talking to him quietly.

"Dammit," Cassie's dad said, his expression relieved as he moved in closer. "What are they saying? What's happening?"

Cassie stepped back to allow the EMTs to work, taking her father with her. Brock stayed by the man's side, working to keep the victim calm and still. All the men who'd helped rescue the guy were drenched, but none of them appeared to even notice.

Brock barked out orders to the paramedics and, working together, they got the injured man on the gurney, covered him in blankets, then got him up the stairs and loaded him into the ambulance. Brock hopped into the back of the rig alongside his patient, and the doors closed. A minute later, the ambulance pulled out of the lot, lights going, sirens silent.

"Everyone in town is here," Ben said to Cassie. "They won't have any traffic on the road."

Cassie nodded, struck as she always was in emergency situations by the sudden feeling of life's fragility. How short it was.

Too short sometimes. Deep in thought, she said good-bye to her dad and then left the pier and drove home. Well, not home exactly, she reminded herself.

Brock's home.

She went outside and sat, staring into the moonlit water, pulling out her cell phone to call the hospital and check on the injured man. But she wasn't his physician or a family member, so they wouldn't give her any information. She checked the next best source—the town's social media page. And sure enough, Ben Murphy was already on the case:

Thanks to swift, heroic measures, a man was saved tonight.

According to reports, the victim fell off the pier into Buzzards Bay, hitting his head in the process. The man would have drowned if not for the three brave souls who dived into Buzzards Bay after him: Wyckford General's new neurosurgeon Samuel Perkins, flight care paramedic Tate Griffin, and Dr. Brock Turner.

Having run my own fishing vessel for over forty years and having seen many maritime close calls, I must say how impressed I was with their efforts. Well done, mates.

The unnamed man, visiting friends in Wyckford, is at the hospital now, suffering a mild concussion, sprained ankle and probably a few sore ribs.

Thanks, Dr. Turner and all. You are heroes.

Unnamed sir, get well soon. And stay off our pier!

Cassie shook her head and went into the guesthouse, changing and then crawling into bed, hoping wherever Brock was, he had at least gotten some dry clothes.

She fell into a deep, dreamless sleep with no idea how long she was out until she woke suddenly, heart pounding in the dark. She peered at her cell phone on the nightstand.

Midnight.

A soft knock sounded on her door, and Cassie got up and padded barefoot across the room to peer out the peephole. Dark, disheveled hair. Shadowed eyes. Scrubs. Cassie's heart kicked hard as she opened the door to a clearly exhausted Brock.

CHAPTER EIGHTEEN

HE'D TOLD HIMSELF, when he left the ER, to go home and go straight to bed. He needed the sleep. And after their talk tonight, leaving things be between them was for the best. But his body got its wires crossed, and Brock ended up at the guesthouse instead.

Cassie answered his knock with a sleep-flushed face and crazy hair, wearing a little tank top and boxers. Brow furrowed and eyes concerned, she asked, "How's the victim?"

He didn't want to talk about the guy from the pier. They didn't have enough time left for that. But if there was a way to say that without sounding like a complete ass, he didn't have the brain capacity to find the words. "He's got a concussion and sore ribs, but he'll be okay."

"That's what my dad said on Facebook too," she said. "Are you okay? You must be dead on your feet. Come in. My bed's warm."

He raised his head and looked into her eyes. "Are you sure?"

"Of course." He took a step, crowding into her space, and she held her ground, sliding a hand up his chest, hooking it around his neck.

Brock didn't remember moving, but then he had her up against the wall, his arms tight around her, her legs around his waist. Even if everything else between them fell apart, there was this. Always this.

Cassie knew it was crazy doing this tonight. There was so much left unsettled, so much left unsaid, for her anyway, but she couldn't stop herself. Especially if this would all be gone soon. She wanted him tonight. Needed him tonight.

Both naked, Brock put on a condom then pressed her into the mattress, the sure and solid weight of his body as comforting as it was arousing. The urgent energy behind his movements resonating within her as well.

It felt more right than anything she'd ever experienced. *He* felt right.

He came up on his forearms, his eyes locked on hers as he slowly pushed inside her. Unable to keep still, she arched up with a soft gasp.

"So good," he murmured, then lowered himself again, his hands sliding up her back and pulling her in close. "Always so good with you."

He brushed his lips over hers, his eyes never leaving her face as he moved inside her.

She sobbed when she climaxed, feeling his release hit him too. Afterward, he pulled her in tight and held her close, tangled in the damp sheets. Cassie couldn't have moved to save her life.

Brock let out a long, slow breath and relaxed. Finally. It gave her a surge of feminine satisfaction that she'd given him that at least.

"Hmm," he said in a voice so low on the register that she could barely hear it. "What are you smiling about?"

Cassie snuggled in closer, stroking a hand down his back. "Brock?"

"Yeah?"

"You were amazing tonight." She shook her head, moved again at the memory. "Never forget that."

Hours later, Brock knew he needed to get up, but lying there with Cassie felt so good. Too good. Especially when they both knew it was almost over.

This shouldn't keep happening, and yet it did. And each time, his feelings got deeper.

All the more reason to stop.

He glanced over at the clock on the nightstand. Three o'clock. Brock moved carefully to avoid waking Cassie. She still murmured in soft protest, and he stroked the hair off her face. She let out a sexy little purr and fell back into a deep sleep. He managed to untangle himself and rolled out of the bed without disturbing her again.

As he moved around the room, searching for the scrubs he'd carelessly discarded earlier, his gaze kept wandering back to her.

The woman he'd fallen in love with against his wishes and all their promises to the contrary.

The woman who cared for him and his daughter but didn't love them.

Not enough to stay anyway.

It was fine. It was her decision. He'd learn to live with it.

When he was dressed, Brock bent over and kissed Cassie gently on the lips. "'Night."

She let out a small snore that made him smile as he left the guesthouse, carefully locking the door behind him. He entered the main house and moved down the hall. Adi was sound asleep. Riley's door was open, and he found his sister sitting in her wheelchair at her bedroom window, staring out into the dark night.

"Hey," he said, startled to see her up, since she had to be nearly as tired as he was from work. Something was obviously wrong. Not that she'd tell him.

"No shift tonight?" he asked carefully.

"Finished early. Now I'm just thinking about things."

"What kinds of things?"

She sighed, then turned to face him. "I wonder sometimes if it's worth it."

"If what's worth it?"

She stared at him and then shook her head. "How hard I try to make life work for me now."

His chest ached, and he drew a slow, painful breath. "Riley, I know it's been hard since the accident, adjusting to all the changes, but you're the best radiology tech I know. And yes, it's worth it. You're worth it."

She shrugged. "Maybe."

"No maybe about it." He sat on the edge of her bed and asked quietly, "What if it was me in your position? What would you tell me?"

"Well, first I'd tell you to stop being such a stubborn pain in the ass," she said, flashing a glimpse of her old smile—the sunny, snarky, confident one she'd shown so freely before the accident. Then she sighed. "Then I'd probably tell you to stop feeling sorry for yourself."

"Okay," he said. "Consider yourself told."

"How well do you know Sam Perkins?"

"The neurosurgeon?" Brock frowned. Honestly, not that well. He seemed nice and competent enough, from what he'd seen, but Brock was usually so busy at the practice he had no time for meet and greets with new hospital staff. "He seems all right. Why?"

"No reason." Riley shrugged. "He asked me out for coffee."

Oh. He'd thought a lot about his sister getting back out into the dating scene again after her injuries, being a protective older brother. But she was a grown woman, and the truth was, he couldn't stop her. And he did understand her need to prove her independence—to herself and everyone else. He really did. He was just terrified for her. Especially after how things had ended up between him and Cassie. The last thing he wanted was for his sister to be heartbroken. "Do you like him?"

"I'm not sure." She smiled slowly. "But coffee can't hurt, right?"

"I guess not."

Since there was nothing to say, he got up to leave.

"Brock?"

He looked back. "Yeah?"

"Thanks."

He was so surprised that she could have knocked him over with a feather.

"For?" Brock asked warily.

"For everything."

CHAPTER NINETEEN

WEDNESDAY MORNING WENT so smoothly at the office that Brock got an actual lunch break for a change. He went to the Buzzy Bird and took a seat at a booth in the corner for some privacy. He wanted a little quiet time to relax before his busy afternoon schedule.

Every day could be like this once you sign the contract...

Brock ate his chicken sandwich, then returned to the office, only to find his waiting room calm and quiet. The front desk was calm and quiet. Everything was calm and quiet.

"There's no patients for me?" he asked Monica, concerned. He eyed the roster. "What about Mrs. B?"

"Oh, she's rescheduled. She had some arthritic flare-up."

Brock was stunned. Mrs. B. had never missed an appointment with him. "And Lisa Boyles?

She was bringing in her three kids for sports physicals."

"They went to the redi-clinic at Wyckford General instead."

"Oh." He felt a little off center. Considering how nuts things normally were, he should enjoy this rare downtime. "I'll go get some charting done."

"Sure."

But when he got to his office and sat down, the charting didn't appeal. Where was a fast-paced ER shift when he needed one? He saw patients that afternoon, but it remained quiet and sedate. Not at all what he was used to.

At first, he'd thought that signing the contract would be the answer to everything. Free up his time and he could spend more of it with his daughter, get his personal life back in order. Except now that he'd gotten a taste of what it could be like—the world going on without him, all on its own—he wasn't sure if he liked it.

That night for the first time in months, Brock got home in time for dinner. He walked into his house and blinked. His living room had been turned into a fort. Blankets and sheets were stretched across the couches and tucked into the entertainment center, into shelves, anywhere and everywhere. He crouched down, and yep, it was filled with what appeared to be every single toy Winnie owned.

He entered the kitchen to find Adi and Cassie sitting at the table, eating chocolate cupcakes. Brock met Cassie's gaze, and the air did that unique crackle thing while her slow smile brought back memories of the night before.

"Daddy, *cupcakes*!" Adi said.

"I'm sorry." Brock pretended to scrub out his ear. "Was that *English*?"

His daughter grinned.

Brock pulled Adi into his arms for a hug and came away a little sticky. "You're supposed to eat the cupcake, not bathe in it."

This earned him another grin. "Try it!"

Adi held one out to him.

Brock took a bite, and he had to admit that the soft, spongy chocolate confection was amazing. He took another bite, pretending to go for Adi's fingers, earning him a belly laugh.

Best sound ever. He started laughing as well. Brock turned and found Cassie watching them with a wistful look in her eyes, which she hid fast. "Hope you don't mind," she said. "It's a backward dinner."

"We *love* backward dinners!" Adi said.

They'd never had a backward dinner.

Winnie sat on the floor at Adi's feet, begging and whining.

"She's sad 'cause Cassie said dogs can't have chocolate," Adi said. "Chocolate's bad for them. They go like this…" She mimed choking, complete with sound effects, before "dying."

"Nice," Brock said.

Winnie whined.

"Don't feel bad for the puppy," Cassie told Brock. "She got her dessert too."

"She ate a bag of powdered sugar," Adi said.

Brock looked at the tiny dog. "When you say bag of powdered sugar…"

"The *entire* bag, including the paper." Cassie shook her head. "She has no self control."

They all looked at the dog, who snorted, then burped, emitting a little puff of white.

"You gonna eat with us, Daddy?" Adi asked. "We're having mac and cheese!"

"My favorite," Brock said dryly.

Adi grinned. "No, it's *my* favorite."

Brock glanced at the unopened box of mac and cheese on the counter and grimaced. "Did Lois come today?"

"She did!" Adi said. "She packed my lunch!"

Now that his daughter had started using English again, apparently she spoke in all exclamation points.

"C'mon. Join us," Cassie said, her voice a little husky now, reminding Brock of how she sounded the night before. He cleared his throat and looked at the box again. "What are you afraid of?"

"Clogged arteries."

Cassie pointed to the half-empty bag of baby carrots next to the mac and cheese. "We've got veggies too."

"Adi doesn't like carrots."

"I do so!" Adi picked up a carrot and dipped it in a bowl of what looked like salad dressing before jamming it into her mouth, dripping dressing everywhere.

Brock let out a breath.

Cassie looked at him, amused. "It's nonfat vanilla yogurt."

He shuddered at that combination but couldn't object. "Where's Riley?"

"Hospital for a shift. How was work?"

In the past, the answer to this question would have been "crazy." But that didn't apply today. "Quiet."

"That's good for a change, right?"

He shrugged. Honestly, Brock still felt discombobulated at how easily his world had gone on without him. And if it was that quiet now, imagine when Cassie was gone…

Maybe signing that contract wasn't such a great idea after all.

His chest ached as he looked at the box of mac and cheese. He needed more fortification than simple carbs to think all this through, so he went to the freezer and pulled out a couple of steaks. While he defrosted them in the microwave, he headed out the back door and started the grill. He'd bought it two years ago and never used it once, but it started right up.

Cassie stood in the open door watching him. "Feeling manly?"

"I'm feeling something."

She smiled and walked closer to him. "Ready for the surgery tomorrow?"

"Yep."

And while he'd gone over Serene's files and his notes for the procedure in the morning, he'd tried not to think too much past that. Because then Cassie would be gone, and all this domestic bliss would be over.

Don't get used to it, he told himself.

But how could he not? How could he not savor her standing there looking warm and soft and so sexy it hurt?

Then Winnie barreled out the back door, chased by Adi and her droid, both heading right for Cassie, full speed ahead.

Brock stepped in front of Cassie to intervene, bearing the brunt of the inevitable impact, bending low to grab for the puppy just as Adi swung her toy and—

It collided hard with Brock's head. He staggered back and tripped over Winnie. The puppy yelped, and Brock shifted his weight, but the dog wound its way between his legs. He lost his balance, falling and hitting the ground with teeth-jarring impact, smacking his head on the concrete. Stars burst behind his eyeballs, then... nothing.

CHAPTER TWENTY

"Brock?"

The urgent voice came from far away and old habit had him responding. He blinked his eyes open, then immediately wished he hadn't as pain sliced through his head, making him want to vomit.

"Brock. Can you hear me?" Cassie said, her tone purely professional now.

He closed his eyes again. "Adi—"

Cassie knelt at his side. "She's fine. The dog's fine. We're all fine. Now please open your eyes and talk to me. Can you tell me your name and what day it is?"

Hell, no. If he opened his eyes, he'd definitely puke.

If the barking didn't split open his head first.

"Quiet, Winnie," Cassie said, all calm efficiency. "Adi, can you take the dog inside and put her in the laundry room, please? While I call 911."

Brock did open his eyes then. "No ambulance."

"You lost consciousness, Brock. You could have a concussion," Cassie told him.

"*I'm* a doctor too, remember?" he said, then groaned. "What the hell did I hit, a Mack truck?"

Cassie held him down when he tried to sit up, her strength surprising him. "Stay put."

"I'm fine." Except she had two heads. And her lovely hazel eyes were filled with concern.

Brock was used to doing the worrying. He was good at it. The best...

Not anymore.

He stewed on that until his heavy eyes closed again.

Dealing with an emergency in a hospital setting was one thing. Dealing with the man she loved unconscious on the ground before her was something else entirely. Cassie's heart was in her throat as she ran her fingers through Brock's hair, searching for a skull fracture. She found a goose-egg-sized lump at the back of his head, and panic slid down her spine. She checked his vitals—pulse and breathing both normal, but that could change at any moment, depending on the severity of his concussion. She'd just pulled her phone from her pocket when Riley rolled through the back door in her wheelchair.

"Hey, I'm ho—" She stopped, eyes going wide. "What happened?"

"Your brother fell and hit his head." Cassie handed Riley her phone. "Can you call 911, please?"

"On it," Riley said.

Brock stirred again, despite Cassie holding him down. It was like trying to corral a stubborn mule. Eventually she gave up, sitting back on her heels as he clambered to his unsteady feet.

"Brock, please—" Cassie said, straightening to take his arm.

"Ice," he said, snatching Cassie's phone from his sister's hand. "I just need some ice."

"Coming right up, bro." Riley went to the kitchen.

Brock allowed Cassie to lead him over to the porch swing, then sank down onto it, looking like his world was spinning.

"Brock, please let me take you to the ER so they can check you out," Cassie said.

He was green and getting greener, his skin covered in a fine sheen of sweat. Wincing, Brock glanced over to where Adi stood nearby, silent and somber, clutching her droid in two little fists. He managed a weak smile for her. "I'm fine, sweetie. No worries. Daddy's okay."

At that, Adi smiled a little, revealing the gap in the front where she'd lost her tooth.

"You need to be examined, Brock."

"I'm fine."

To prove her point, Cassie held up her hand in front of his face. "How many fingers am I holding up?"

He focused with what appeared to be great effort. "Two."

Lucky guess, and they both knew it.

Riley returned with the ice, wrapped in a towel, and Brock placed it on the back of his thick noggin and settled more carefully on the swing, eyes closed. "Hey, sweetie," he said to Adi. "Why don't you go inside and watch your cartoons? Riley can put them on for you."

Adi ran back into the house, followed by a reluctant Riley. "Stop being an idiot, bro," she said to Brock. "Go get checked out. You of all people know the dangers."

When she was gone, Cassie moved in again. "How are you feeling? Headache? Nausea? What year is it?"

He didn't answer any of her questions, instead asking one of his own. "How long was I out?"

"I'd say around thirty seconds, maybe a bit longer."

"Then I'm good. I just need to sit here for a bit."

"Brock—"

"Water," he said. "Can you get me a glass of water, please?"

What Cassie wanted to get him was into the car for a ride to the ER, but seeing how difficult that would be on her own, she went instead went to the kitchen to fill a glass for him, keeping one eye on Brock through the window, while checking on Adi and Riley with the other. They were sitting on the sofa in the living room with the puppy, watching cartoons.

When she returned outside, he hadn't moved a single inch as far as she could tell. His big, long body was stretched out in his seat, his head back, cushioned on the ice behind him.

Far too still.

Cassie set the glass down and crouched at his side, checking his pulse again.

Still normal, thank goodness.

Brock jerked, swore, then sent her a dark look.

"Sorry," she said on a relieved breath. "You were so still. I thought..." She shook her head. "I brought your water."

He took it with a shaky hand and gulped some down while Cassie took a seat beside him, a new concern arising.

"With your injury, I can't allow you to assist with the surgery in the morning. There's too much risk for the patient," she said.

"I'm—" Brock started, then stopped, apparently coming to the same conclusion. "I can observe."

"Yes, you can." She got up and grabbed her phone from where Brock had tossed it earlier. "I'll need to get a replacement and brief them on what's happening before tomorrow morning."

She sighed, then dialed the hospital and told them what had happened. They promised to find another surgeon to assist her ASAP, then ended the call. Eventually, after checking Brock again to make sure he wasn't going to expire on her any time soon, Cassie helped him inside and got him some aspirin for the pain. Then, she started dinner.

By the time they'd eaten and Cassie had consulted with her new surgical assistant for the morning, arranging to meet them half an hour before the surgery to go over everything in person, it was after nine. She put Adi to bed, then moved down the hall to Brock's bedroom to check on him again. It had been an every-two-hours thing since his injury, per protocol. She'd wake him up, ask him his name and the date, check his vitals, then let him sleep again.

His room was dark now, but she'd left the bathroom light on. Brock lay sprawled on his stomach, face turned away. Cassie turned on the lights, then sat on the edge of the bed, gliding her fingers over his forehead, brushing his hair back.

Brock sighed. "You were just here."

"Two hours ago. How's the nausea?"

"Cassie, I'm fine. Go away."

"What's your name?"

He let out a long breath. "Ticked off and trying to sleep."

"Funny. Follow my finger."

He smacked her hand away from his face.

"Stop being a baby," she told him. "If one of your patients acted like this, you'd—"

"Assume they were good to go."

His hair was damp from his shower earlier. She'd advised him against it, given the risk of a fall, but again, he'd been a stubborn ass and done it anyway. Luckily, he'd been fine, which was good since she had no idea how she'd have moved a two-hundred-pound, wet, unconscious male. There would have been paramedics involved for sure.

He'd pulled on a pair of sweatpants, barely. They sat indecently low on his hips, giving her a good look at his broad back, a pair of twin dimples at the top of his buttocks, and a hint of the lightning bolt tattoo she'd had fun exploring the other night.

Man, I'm going to miss all this so much. Miss him...

"Why are you still here?"

"You have a probable concussion," she reminded him. "As a physician, I can't leave you alone. It's unethical."

"*Mild* concussion. Jesus. And as a fellow physician, I'm telling you to stop hovering."

He let out a long-suffering breath. It hadn't escaped her that he hadn't moved. And he was looking extremely tense, his muscles rock hard with strain, which she confirmed by stroking her hand along his back and feeling the knots of stress there.

Leaning over him, using two hands, Cassie began working the tension from his shoulders. He might not allow her to take him in for treatment, but she could at least make him more comfortable here. "Tell me what I can do for you."

He let out a muffled groan into his pillow. "Don't stop that. Ever."

She smiled, even as her chest ached. Unfortunately, she wouldn't have a choice when she went back to California. Which was too bad since touching him was pure pleasure. His skin was warm, smooth, and he smelled so good that she wanted to snuggle into him and stay there forever. Since that wasn't possible, she concentrated on the treatment protocol again. His eyes were closed, but she checked the lump on his head and saw no sign of further swelling or bleeds. "Are you still dizzy? How's the head-ache?"

"No and better," he said. His voice held frustration and affection. "I'm fine."

"Okay, but I'm keeping an eye on you," she said, just as frustrated and affectionate. "I'll stay here tonight, just in case. And I'll be back to check on you in a few hours."

CHAPTER TWENTY-ONE

"BROCK?"

He had no idea how much later it was when he heard Cassie whisper his name. Odd that the day before, hearing her voice turned him on, and now he wanted to strangle her. *"No."*

"It's 5:30 a.m. I'm heading to the hospital to start prepping for Serene's surgery."

He pried open one eye, noted the clock on his nightstand, then closed it again.

"Brock."

He sighed and rolled to his back. "Okay. I'm awake."

She sank to the bed at his hip and put her hand on his bare chest. Her fingers stroked him lightly, and his annoyance abruptly faded.

"How are you feeling?" she asked.

"I know my name, and I'm not hot or cold. I'm just right."

"Can you follow my finger?"

"Cassie, I have a finger for you."

She sighed. "Fine. I'll see you at the hospital."

He knew he should get up and go with her, but her touch felt so good that he didn't want to move. In fact, he fell asleep again. And when he woke up, it was past noon. Way past Serene's surgery and way past him observing anything except how late it was.

Dammit.

With a growl, he got up and was happy to find the room didn't spin around him anymore. The lump on the back of his head still hurt, but the swelling had gone down, and he felt steadier on his feet. The worst was over. He'd closed the office today, thinking he'd be at the hospital for Serene's surgery, so he had nowhere to be.

He got ready, then walked into the kitchen to find a note from Lois saying she needed more cleaning supplies, and he needed to order them. Brock fixed himself a cup of coffee and some toast, then sat down at the table to do just that on his phone. With the supplies ordered, he texted Cassie, asking her how the surgery had gone.

When she arrived home a few hours later, Brock was ready to climb the walls. As a man used to staying busy, this sitting around and waiting crap was for the birds.

Cassie walked in wearing a pair of scrubs from the hospital, looking tired, but happy.

"Good," she said as he got up and pulled her

into his arms. "She came through the procedure fine and all the prosthetics worked well, and the neurosurgeon thinks she should regain use of most of the reattached nerves in her face with time. The maxillofacial surgeons are just finishing up their final touches now, then she'll go to recovery. It's been a long eight hours though."

"I bet." He held her and rocked her, pride swelling in his chest. "You're amazing, Cassie."

"Thanks," she said into his chest, making him smile.

He might not have Cassie forever, but she was here with him now and that's what mattered. "You nauseous?"

She wrinkled her nose at him. "Huh?"

"What's your name?"

She blinked, then narrowed her eyes. "You're making fun of me. I was seriously concerned last night, you know, and—"

"Are you feverish?" He pressed his lips to her temple. "Nope." He stroked a hand down her throat to her chest, pushing the V-neck of her scrubs aside with his fingers.

"What are you doing?" she asked.

"Seeing if you're getting a chill."

"By copping a feel?"

He smiled and lowered his head, kissing her.

She arched against him, her fingers gliding into his hair and over the lump on the back of his head. Which made him hiss in pain. "Oh, God, I'm sorry."

Keeping a hold of her, he tugged off her scrub shirt. "Always."

She frowned. "Always what?"

"You always make me feel better." He cupped a breast through her bra.

She made a sound of pure arousal even as she shook her head. "Brock—"

He pulled her close to kiss her again.

Cassie said shakily, "You're not up for this."

Gripping her hips, he ground against her, showing her exactly how "up" he was.

"Seriously. You need to rest today, not—"

"I'm going to be very still." He picked her up then, carrying her down the hall to his bedroom, where he stripped them both and laid her on the bed while he reached into his nightstand drawer for a condom. After he'd put it on, he climbed atop the mattress. This time, Cassie rolled him beneath her and took charge. He ran his hands along her sweet thighs as she rose and took him inside her.

Then she pulled his hands away from her and lifted them to the headboard above his head. "You have to stay very still, remember?"

Brock opened his eyes to find her face only inches from his. Bright hazel eyes stared down at him, and his breath lodged in his throat. She let go of his hands and skimmed her fingers down his shoulders and chest to his stomach, then back up again as she rode him slowly, their gazes locked.

This felt like more than sex, more than their usual connection.

This felt like love.

Cassie's hips rocked, and she nipped gently at his lips, nothing guarded or shielded in her gaze, nothing held back. He saw everything in her eyes, all she felt and all she wanted, the same as him, even if it was impossible.

She was going easy, but he needed more. If this was their last time together, he wanted to sear this memory into his brain forever. Brock rocked up, changing the angle, creating a deeper penetration. Inhaling sharply, Cassie bowed over him, entwining her fingers with his as they kissed, her muscles quivering as the pressure built. Lost in her, Brock whispered her name.

Cassie skittered over the edge, her entire body shuddering in gorgeous relief above him, and he groaned as the wave took him under right along with her.

Sometime later Cassie opened her eyes and nearly jumped a foot.

Adi was nose to nose with her.

So was Winnie.

The little girl was leaning over the bed. The dog was on top of Cassie.

At least until she moved. With a reproachful look, the French bulldog rolled aside like a boneless glob. Cassie glanced over at Brock, who was asleep flat on his stomach, sprawled out, and thankfully covered by the blanket.

Adi smiled at Cassie. "Whatcha doing in Daddy's bed? Are you having a sleepover?"

"Uh…" She tried not to eyeball Brock's sweatpants on the floor behind Adi as she reached for a book on the nightstand, improvising, thinking that was better than explaining a post-surgery booty call to a five-year-old. "Reading him a bedtime story."

"It's not bedtime," the girl said, frowning.

"Oh, well…" She had Cassie there. Thankfully, Brock groaned beside her.

"Hey, sweetie," he said, opening his eyes. "Hungry?"

"Yeah!"

"Is Lois still here?" Brock asked, then glanced at the clock. "Never mind. Why don't you get one of those cupcakes you made for a snack?"

"Okay!" Adi ran for the door with the puppy on her heels.

When they were gone, Cassie covered her face. "Oh, God."

"She didn't see anything."

Cassie stood with the sheet wrapped around her. "I know, but this was part of our agreement and now she's seen us in bed together and—"

Brock propped himself up on his side, looking way sexier than any man had a right to. "I think we can safely say our agreement is shot to hell by now, even before this."

Cassie let the sheet drop as she tugged on her panties and scrub pants and bra, then searched for her top, remembering too late that it was out in the living room. *Crap*. Then she glanced at herself in the mirror over his dresser and groaned. Hair: wild. Lips: swollen. Face: flushed.

He got up too, sans sheet.

"What are you doing?" she hissed. "Put some clothes on!"

"Stop shouting." He winced then strode over, butt naked, to grab his sweats from the floor and pull them on.

His brow was furrowed. His mouth was tight. There were shadows under his eyes. He was holding it together—the guy knew no other way—but he clearly felt awful.

"Take it easy. I'll take care of Adi after I get an update on Serene."

"No. I've got it."

"You're still sick."

"I'm fine. Besides, I need to get used to doing

this on my own again. Since I'm off today, I'll take her to the pier. We'll play arcade games and eat junk food."

I need to get used to doing this on my own again...

The words sliced Cassie open like a scalpel, even though they were true. Soon, if everything went well with her patient's recovery she'd be back in sunny San Diego and Brock would be here in Wyckford with his daughter and his sister and their adorable dog. An image of them running on the pier, looking like a real family, made her chest ache. It was everything she'd never known she'd wanted. And it was vanishing before her eyes. She swallowed hard against the lump in her throat and said the first thing that came into her head. "You're a good dad."

He didn't have any obvious reaction, but Cassie knew her words had touched him. The thought that he didn't hear it enough made her heart melt. Not the fleeting kind of melting either. The lasting kind that made her want to burrow into him and never let go. Which was a problem.

A huge, messy problem. Because people were depending on her to get back to California.

Which in turn reminded her that she needed to call her partners in the practice later and let them know how the surgery had gone. If things continued on the same trajectory they had when Cassie had left the hospital earlier, they'd be thrilled. She was thrilled too, both for the results of their new technology and for Serene.

Brock went into the bathroom and closed the door. Cassie pulled on one of his T-shirts, then headed out toward the living room, surrounded by Brock's scent, her heart filled to brimming with love and the pain of impending loss, wondering how in the world she'd survive when this was all over and there'd be no reason to see him again.

CHAPTER TWENTY-TWO

THE FOLLOWING WEEK was the Fourth of July in Wyckford, and Brock was back in the ER, trying to keep his mind on his patients, which wasn't easy. Especially since he'd checked in on Serene earlier and she had recovered enough to be discharged that afternoon, just in time for the big fireworks celebration that night on the pier. She was doing amazing, and he was so happy for her. And so sad for himself.

Cassie had transformed the woman's injuries and restored her to the beautiful person Serene had been before the accident. And yes, there would be weeks more of healing before all the bandages came off and she was fully recovered, but the results were already remarkable.

Unfortunately, Cassie had transformed Brock's life too. From drab and drudgery, to bright and sparkling and one full of possibilities. He wasn't sure how he'd go back again. But he'd have to. Because even as he worked, Cassie was back at the guesthouse, packing up her things to return to California. He'd promised himself not to get emotionally involved and he'd ended up falling completely and hopelessly in love.

And sure, he'd always known Cassie would leave when the case was over and return to San Diego. But that wasn't the point. The point was that it wouldn't be the same.

Brock spent the next five hours working, and at the end of his shift, all he wanted was to crash. That's when Nurse Madison caught up to him in the hallway of the hospital, wearing pink scrubs, hair up, looking a little frazzled. "Got a minute?"

The ER had been a mess all day. Besides the usual heart attacks, hangovers and expected fireworks injuries, there'd been a five-car pileup on the highway and a mob of strep throat infections. But his trusty nurse had kept up with Brock every step of the way. "For you, always."

Madi smiled. "Aw. Thanks." Then her smile faded. "You know Cassie is flying out tonight?"

He let out a breath. "Yeah, I know."

"And what are you going to do about that?"

Brock scowled. "Me?"

"Yes, you!" Madi shook her head like he was as thick as a brick. "Everyone with eyeballs can see you two are perfect for each other, Brock.

It's all over your face. It's all over the way you act with her. Cassie too."

"I don't act any different with her than I do with everyone else," he said.

"Really?"

"Yes," he muttered. *No.*

But she wasn't listening. She continued ranting. "Seriously? The whole town has seen that kiss picture on the social media page. And the other too, with you guys at Adi's award ceremony." She smacked his arm. "C'mon. For a doctor, you're kind of dumb. You two need to discuss this and make some choices before it's too late. You're crazy about Cassie. You even let yourself depend on her. You, the King of Depending on No One!"

Brock wasn't afraid of much, but even he knew to be afraid of Madison when her eyes were crazy like they were now, so he said nothing. She drew a deep breath and studied him, hands on hips. "Let me just say this. I know it seems impossible, with you here on the East Coast and her on the West, but sometimes love just works out." She huffed a minute. "Miracles happen."

"Miracles?" He pinched the bridge of his nose. "Look, it's late. I'm tired. *You're* tired. Did you need a minute to tell me something important or just to yell at me?"

She sighed. "I also wanted to know if you could pick up a shift at the free clinic this week."

"Depends on if I have someone to watch Adi, since Cassie won't be here anymore."

"Right." Madi sighed and got quiet again. "I keep telling myself something's going to happen. That she won't leave and somehow you guys will have a happily-ever-after. It's been so great having her back home again, you know?"

Yeah, he did know. He knew because he felt the same way. The thought of Cassie not being in Wyckford made his heart hurt. But how could he ask her to give up everything for him?

He couldn't. That was the problem.

Which proved Madison's point, of course. He *was* crazy about Cassie and had been since that first day on the beach. He'd told her how he felt, showed her in every way he could think of, and it still wasn't enough. In the beginning, he'd mistakenly believed she needed him. That he was the one doing *her* the favor by letting her stay in his guesthouse.

He'd been wrong. Very wrong.

Cassie was the center of her own universe. She wasn't dependent on anyone. She would never be one more thing on any man's plate to take care of. Especially since the truth was that *she'd* been taking care of him and Adi since day one. "I'm going home now," he said. "Unless you want to hit me again."

"Do I need to?" she asked.

"No."

Madison studied him for a long beat, then surprised Brock by hugging him tight. "It's okay to be stupid in love," she assured him, patting him like he wasn't a head and a half taller than her. "Especially after all you've been through," she said, this last word spoken in a definite warning tone. "But then you have to wise up and figure it out. Don't let this second chance at happiness slip through your hands because you're scared."

Then she was out the door before he could respond. He wasn't scared.

Am I?

When Kylie had died, he'd thought she'd taken the best part of him with her. But from the moment Cassie had returned to his life, she'd reawakened him from the inside out. She'd given him back his heart, his soul, his happiness. One day at a time. She'd given him back everything.

And hell yeah, he was scared. Terrified of losing it all again.

But Madi was right about something else too. He had a choice to make.

Let that fear rule him and his decisions, or go for it.

Something new was blooming in his chest, overtaking the terror.

Certainty. Security. Resolution.

Since Cassie had returned to his life, he'd felt like a family again with Adi and Riley. Hell, even Winnie. A real family. That was all Cassie. And, like an idiot, he'd been ready to let it all go, just because it would be hard. And risky. Well, to hell with that.

Lord knew he could do hard. He'd been doing hard for five years now.

And for Cassie, he'd do hard forever if it meant they could be together.

They'd figure the rest out.

First though, he had to find her and tell her before it was too late.

Cassie was still at the guesthouse, on a Zoom call with the partners in her practice, filling them in on Serene's remarkable progress and the success of their METAMORPHOSIS technology. She relayed all the pertinent data and measurements, the before and after slides, and the video clips from during the surgery, showing Cassie placing the prosthetics that had been custom-made by the team in California for her patient.

"Fantastic news, Cassie," said Dr. Ongulla, one of the chief partners. "We expected you to do well with this, but I had no idea how wonderful it would turn out."

"Agreed," said Dr. Chin. "With this data set, we'll definitely be able to move forward in other areas of reconstruction as well."

"And speaking of moving forward—" this came from Dr. Allende, the other chief partner in the practice "—I'd like to discuss a new opportunity with you."

"Oh." Cassie shifted in her seat. Everything felt so up in the air in her life, between work and Brock and the ache inside her because she'd be leaving him behind. "I'm not sure—"

"Please just hear us out," Dr. Ongulla said.

"Okay."

"As you know, we've discussed opening a second office here in San Diego for a while now, due to our patient load."

Yeah, Cassie knew that. They'd discussed it, ad nauseam, the past few months. And, while she was happy the practice was doing so well, it would make her schedule even more nuts because of the commute.

"Well, since you've been gone, we've discussed it more and have some new ideas."

Her stomach dropped. "What kind of ideas?"

Dr. Allende smiled. "Bicoastal."

"Bicoastal?"

"Yes," Dr. Chin answered, clearly excited

about the topic. "I said, 'Why open another office here, when we can expand to a whole new place?'"

Cassie could think of several off the top of her head, the first of which being cost and the second being the logistical nightmare of scouting locations and securing property. Still, she didn't want to rain on their parade just yet. "Go on."

"And we think the Boston area would be great for a second location," Dr. Ongulla said. "In fact, we think your current location of Wyckford would be perfect. Low property costs. Ease of travel to Boston, if necessary. Top-notch hospital facilities in place already, as evidenced by your work with your patient these past few weeks."

"And since you're familiar with the area and the people there, we think you should head the operation," Dr. Chin added. "What do you think?"

Taken aback, Cassie blinked at her screen. They wanted to open a new practice here, in Wyckford? And have her run it? That would be... That would be wonderful, actually. It would certainly solve all her issues. She could keep an eye on her dad. She could keep an eye on Brock and Adi and Riley and all her friends.

They could be together. They could be a family.

"Yes!" she said, before she could second-guess anything. "I would love that!"

"Great," Dr. Ongulla said. "Sit tight there then until after the holiday. We'll have another conference call the day after tomorrow to discuss things further. And happy Independence Day, Cassie. Well done on the success of your surgery."

After the call ended, Cassie sat there for a moment, just taking it all in. Then she got online to cancel her flight. Then she stared at her packed bags by the door, wondering what the hell to do now. She needed to talk to Brock, tell him the good news and ask him if she could stay in his guesthouse longer, at least until they figured out what was happening with the new practice and what she'd be doing next on that project.

She set her laptop aside, got up, slipped on her sandals and headed for the door, thinking she'd go to the hospital to see if she could catch Brock before his shift in the ER ended.

But as she opened the door, she found him striding down the path toward her, like a man on a mission. He'd obviously come from work, still wearing his navy scrubs, his hospital ID hanging around his neck and a determined look on his face. Her heart melted.

He stopped about a foot away from her, crossing his arms as he watched her. "I saw Serene today before she was discharged. Good work, Cassie."

"Thanks." Cassie swallowed hard against the constriction in her throat. "She's doing well. Listen, I just got off a Zoom call with my practice and—"

"Stop." Brock watched her, his blue gaze laser sharp as always, but for an instant, just the briefest of instants, something not quite identifiable flickered. She wanted to see it again, wanted to reach for it or—better yet—have him give it to her willingly.

"I know you need to go," he said quietly, a thread of steel in his voice. "But before you leave, you need to know that I don't want this to be over between us. I don't care how hard or crazy or difficult it might be to stay together. I want to try. I don't want to lose you, Cassie. I love you."

Then, before she realized what was happening, she was in Brock's arms, snug against his solid, warm chest, surrounded by him. She felt breathless, not from the hug, but from the man himself. How he held her tight, as if she were the most precious thing to him, as if he couldn't wait another second to touch her.

She felt the same way. "I'm not leaving."

"Wait. What?" Brock tilted her face up to his, searching her features. "I don't think I heard that right."

Cassie smiled as happy, relieved tears filled

her eyes. For days she'd been torn apart inside, trying to figure out how to have it all and coming up empty. Now, she'd never have to make that awful choice again. Things wouldn't be easy—not with their crazy schedules and Brock's past—but Cassie didn't want easy. She just wanted Brock. And Adi and Winnie and the new little family they could form together. It's all she'd ever wanted, really. To belong, to feel secure, to know she was loved for exactly who she was. And she'd found it. Right back where she'd started.

With this man.

She told him about the practice and the new location and how they wanted her to run it for them because of how well Serene's case had turned out. Finally, when she was done, Brock exhaled and smiled, tracing a finger along her temple, then tucking a strand of hair behind her ear. "When I was at the hospital, Madi mentioned something about miracles. I've never been a believer in that sort of thing, but now I'm starting to wonder."

"Me too."

He gave her a kiss that made her toes curl before pulling back and taking her hand. "C'mon."

"Where are we going?"

"To see the fireworks," he said, leading her to the house to get Adi and Winnie. Riley was already at the pier, he said, with friends from work. Then they were in the car and heading through town, finding a parking spot and racing through the crowds toward the beach, just as the first colorful explosions filled the sky, lighting up the night in Technicolor brilliance.

As Adi and Winnie watched the overhead display in stunned silence, Brock put his arm around Cassie and pulled her into his side. "I love you, Cassie. I think I have since the day you showed up on the beach searching for Winnie, giving me all you had just to help me out. I can't wait to start a future with you."

She held on to his waist, snuggling into his chest. "I love you too. And Adi. And Winnie."

The little dog let out an "arf" in response.

Brock's mouth curved as the night lit up around them. "Yeah?"

Her heart soared. "Oh, yeah."

EPILOGUE

One year later...

CASSIE WOKE FROM a sun-soaked Maui beach snooze when a shadow blocked her rays. She opened her eyes and took in the sight of Brock in nothing but loose board shorts, slung so low on his hips as to be indecent. His big, built body was tanned and wet from his ocean swim and he had a wicked gleam in his gaze.

"Don't," she warned him as he got closer to her. "Don't you dare—"

With a grin, he scooped her out of the oversize lounge chair on the private beach of their honeymoon house and up against his drenched body.

"—get me wet," she finished weakly. Too late.

"Oh, stop complaining, Mrs. Turner." He nuzzled her neck for a moment, then dropped down onto the lounge, with her now on top of him. He made himself comfortable, his hands roaming freely over her body as he did. "Mmm. You smell like a coconut. You know I love coconuts."

She did. She knew this firsthand... It'd been a lovely honeymoon week, and they had a few more days left. They'd gotten married six months ago, but this had been their first opportunity for a getaway, what with the busy practice and all. As their wedding gift, Riley had agreed to watch Adi and Winnie for them. Which was surprising since she had so little free time these days, with her crazy schedule at the hospital and some secret project she was working on with neurosurgeon Sam Perkins, who Riley constantly complained about. From what Cassie understood of the situation, they'd been forced into working together on a case study by the hospital administrator because of Riley's skills as a radiology tech, but she and Sam clashed constantly. Cassie thought maybe there was more going on there than met the eye, but getting information out of Riley, especially about her personal life, was like pulling teeth, so...

Madi and Luna were helping with Adi and Winnie too, between their own busy jobs and busier social lives. Madison had always been the town good girl, devoted to her work and caring for her older mother. A perfectionist, Madi had earned the name Goody Two-shoes in school. But lately, Cassie had seen a different side of her friend—daring, reckless and carefree. Well, as carefree as Madi could be, but still. Cassie wondered if it had something to do with all the time Madi was spending with Brock's friend Tate Griffin, a military flight paramedic who was staying in Wyckford while he was on leave. And trying to catch Luna—between her work as a physical therapist, filling in at the Buzzy Bird when needed and selling her art in town—was proving more difficult as well. Luna wasn't seeing anyone, that Cassie knew about anyway, but things changed on a dime in Wyckford, so you never knew from one day to the next.

Not that they needed her friends' help much with Adi, since Cassie's dad and his new granddaughter had hit it off like a house afire. Winnie too. The three of them were practically inseparable these days. Her dad loved being an instant grandpa and Adi loved having a new playmate who could also take her to fun places and do things with her. Her dad had even taught Winnie some manners. Talk about miracles.

Cassie's new practice was getting closer to the grand opening, though it would be a month or so before that happened. And Brock had finally signed the contract with the hospital and they'd hired on another GP to share the load. Their schedules were still nuts, but they wouldn't have it any other way.

Having so little free time usually, they'd made the most of their alone time here.

And it had been amazing.

Now, Cassie lay atop of Brock in sated, contented quiet. They'd be back to their frenetic pace soon enough and there was plenty of drama in Wyckford to keep them on their toes.

As if reading her thoughts, Brock entwined his fingers with hers and drew them up to his mouth to kiss her palm, then regarded her with a serious look on his face. "Promise me something."

"Anything."

"We'll never get too busy to do this." He kissed her forehead. "Just be together."

Cassie smiled and leaned up to touch her lips to his. "Promise."

* * * * *

If you enjoyed this story, check out these other great reads from Traci Douglass

The GP's Royal Secret
A Mistletoe Kiss in Manhattan
Their Barcelona Baby Bombshell
Island Reunion with the Single Dad

All available now!